Other Titles Available from Otto Penzler's
Classic American Mystery Library

# ACCOUNTING
## for MURDER

*Emma Lathen*

OTTO PENZLER BOOKS

NEW YORK

OTTO
PENZLER
BOOKS

Otto Penzler Books        Simon & Schuster Inc.
129 West 56th Street      Rockefeller Center
New York, NY 10019        1230 Avenue of the Americas
(Editorial Offices only)  New York, NY 10020

First Otto Penzler Books Edition 1995
Published by arrangement with Macmillan Publishing Company

Manufactured in the United States of America

10  9  8  7  6  5  4  3  2  1

Library of Congress Cataloging-in-Publication Data

Lathan, Emma, pseud.
    Accounting for murder / Emma Lathen.—1st Otto Penzler Books ed.
    p.   cm.
    I. Title.
PS3562.A755A64   1995              94-36627  CIP
813'.54—dc20
    ISBN 1-57283-000-X

# Contents

# 1

# Come, Begin

Wall Street is the hub of the financial universe, and not the least imposing of its mighty institutions is the Sloan Guaranty Trust, the third largest bank in the world, with branches in twenty-four countries—rumored to be on the point of acquiring the assets of Wheatman's Mutual. Wheatman's is having slight difficulties these days.

At the Sloan, no place is more important than the sixth floor, home of the Trust Department. Here young men fresh from the Business School coolly phone company presidents to dispute earnings projections; here senior trust officers maintain unencouraging reserve when real estate developers outline million-dollar leasing schemes. At least twice in the past five years, some fairly clever Texas interests have been surprised to find proxy fights shot from under them, on the sixth floor of the Sloan Guaranty Trust.

These complex and momentous operations are directed from behind a door marked: John Putnam Thatcher. Thatcher, senior vice president, is not only director of the Trust Department but—so the scuttlebutt runs—about to be elevated to the eminence of the Investment Division.

Not that any of his subordinates would ask him about this. A youthful sixty, Thatcher has a resilient vigor that is far removed from the frozen dignity exhibited by Bradford Withers, the president of the bank. Yet somehow the members of the Trust Department who argue quite heatedly with

Thatcher about the Sloan's holdings of Bravura Chemicals
do not venture personal questions.

In an institution composed of many important men, he is
—in a relaxed fashion—one of the most important.

Naturally then, while his subordinates wrote six-million-
dollar mortgages or acquired controlling interests in small
steel mills, John Thatcher was coping with a personnel
problem.

"I tell you, John," Everett Gabler repeated with fussy
self-importance, "I can't be responsible for a satisfactory
monthly statement if I'm going to be kept shorthanded. And
I *am* shorthanded when young Nicolls spends all of his time
with Trinkam."

"Yes," Thatcher said wearily. "Yes, I see that."

"I didn't like the arrangement to begin with," Everett continued in tones of strong censure. "I foresaw the very difficulties we are now encountering." Everett Gabler, oldest,
most trusted, and possibly most infuriating of Thatcher's
section chiefs, always foresaw difficulties. "At best it was an
irregular arrangement. But now it develops that Trinkam's
section"—Utilities—"is using Nicolls for more and more
work, and it is certainly unreasonable to say that we"—Rails
and Industrials—"are getting our fair share of his work although he is still being charged to our budget. Why, some
days he doesn't even get in to pick up his mail!"

Thatcher tapped a pencil on his desk. Not a line and staff
man himself, he was prepared to let his senior officers work
out their own arrangements for getting work done. But to
Everett Gabler, haphazard allocation of salary charges, like
the borrowing of secretaries, represented a threat to competent administration. He was in his early fifties but he was
a little old lady—that is, a little old lady who knew a great
deal about Rails and Industrials.

". . . if it goes on, and you know that our budget is already
being stretched almost beyond what could be expected, I
don't see how we can plan our Industrial Survey . . ."

"Eh? What did you say, Everett?" Thatcher roused himself to ask.

"I said that if this goes on, we're going to need another man in Rails and Industrials."

Thatcher considered this. The empire-building propensities of his section chiefs, their insatiable hunger for new men, was a failing from which not even Gabler was immune.

"We'd have to think that over," he temporized, watching Gabler pull off his glasses and polish them while his myopic eyes assumed a cunning squint that indicated several good arguments in favor of immediate recruiting.

In fact, he had opened his mouth to begin his catalogue when the desk buzzer rang.

"Sorry," Thatcher murmured gratefully. "Yes, Miss Corsa?"

"Mr. Robichaux on the line," his secretary announced.

"Put him on . . . Hello, Tom? Good to hear from you!" he said with uncharacteristic heartiness. Gabler frequently had this effect on him. He watched his section chief close his mouth, adjust his glasses precisely on the bridge of a rather long nose, and lean back. Tenacious if nothing else was old Everett, now folding his arms to signify determination to sit out the interruption.

"John!" brayed Robichaux, senior partner of Robichaux and Devane, the investment bankers, and one of the world's boomers. "Glad to have caught you in. Been a long time since we got together, isn't it? What have you been doing with yourself?"

"Nothing much," Thatcher replied, moving the receiver several inches from his ear. "How are you, Tom? And"—he cast about for the name of the current Mrs. Robichaux—"and Dorothy?"

There was a moment of silence on the line, then Robichaux repeated the name—"Dorothy?"—before recognition came: "Oh! Dorothy! Dorothy and I aren't together these days. Thought you knew," he said with no audible regret. Then, possibly feeling he had been abrupt, he expanded. "To tell you the truth, John, I'm having one hell of a time."

Rightly taking this elliptical sentence to refer to the legal and financial difficulties rather than the emotional turmoil connected with Dorothy's departure, Thatcher said something meaningless and vaguely sympathetic while he suppressed a smile at the look of moral indignation assumed by Everett, who could hear every explosive word that Robichaux uttered.

Rails and Industrials would not have tolerated such peccadilloes for one moment. But on the other hand, Robichaux and Devane would have condoned them in no one but a Robichaux. The Devanes were Quakers.

". . . so it's touch and go," shouted Tom cheerfully. It was strange that a man who owned his own yacht was incapable of grasping the fact that the telephone accomplished the transmission. "That's not what I called about, John. I've uncovered an interesting little problem that I thought you might care to look over."

He paused and, when this bait failed, continued in a burst of candor, "The fact is, John, I'm hoping that you'll do me a little favor."

Thatcher braced himself. Since their undergraduate days in Harvard Yard he had convinced himself that it was a mistake to underestimate Robichaux; he might look like a cruise director and behave like an Edwardian buck, but he was, as many an operator in the Street had discovered, a shrewd businessman who had scored several coups solely on the basis of this aggressively simple manner.

"Yes," he replied cautiously, while Gabler, openly listening, narrowed his eyes in suspicion. "Well, Tom, anything I can do for you," he said with slight emphasis on the verb.

Robichaux chuckled. "Mighty careful, aren't you?" he said genially. "I know you'll help, John. Now listen, have you ever heard of a man named Clarence Fortinbras?"

Thatcher searched his memory and found no Fortinbras—outside of *Hamlet*—at all.

"No."

"I see," Robichaux said slowly, pausing for thought before he went on in a slightly lowered voice, "I'm having lunch with him today, and I'd appreciate it very much if you'd join us."

Thatcher would have found no difficulty in ignoring the significant, slightly sinister tone with which this was said—

knowing as he did that it was one of Tom's most successful weapons with women and customers—except for a glance at Gabler. It was now eleven-thirty; a luncheon appointment with Robichaux would not only terminate this conference on Rails and Industrials, it would protect him from a luncheon session that centered on its problems. Gabler was a vegetarian.

"Certainly I'll join you," he told Robichaux. "What is it . . ."

"The thing is," Robichaux interposed in clumsily conspiratorial tones, "we're talking business, and I'd like to fill you in before we meet. What about meeting me at Fraunces Tavern at about twelve-thirty? Fortinbras is coming at one o'clock."

"Fine," Thatcher replied.

"I knew I could count on you," Robichaux said, ringing off.

Thatcher, amused by the eternal small boy in Tom, again faced Gabler.

"Have you ever heard of Clarence Fortinbras?"

Gabler flicked through a filing cabinet mind. *"Fortinbras on Accounts Receivable,"* he declared.

"I beg your pardon?"

"The standard text on accounts receivable," explained Gabler sternly. "I seem to remember that Fortinbras is Clarence."

And if Everett Gabler seemed to remember that Fortinbras of *Fortinbras on Accounts Receivable* was Clarence, then Clarence he was.

What was that old reprobate Robichaux doing with a noted accountant?

". . . and so, John, I think you'll agree with me that we're very short-handed as it is. And with this new account," Gabler was saying with measured disapproval.

John Thatcher again shouldered the burden of high office.

"Well, I'm broadminded to a fault," Tom said, gesturing the waiter for another round of drinks, "But when I caught her with the kennelman, I decided that enough was enough." He glanced around the small dining room of Fraunces Tavern seeking enemy ears, then he leaned forward across the table

to hiss: "It's going to be touch and go, you know. There
are . . . there are complications."

"I see that there might be," Thatcher replied truthfully.
In all the years he had known him, Tom had been involved
in complications; it was only during divorce proceedings that
they assumed any importance. Thatcher watched him assume
an expression of extreme virtue.

"Old Barnwell says I'll have to watch my step, but he
thinks we may get through it without losing too much,"
Robichaux said. Barnwell (of Barnwell and McBridge) had
probably not put it so tactfully, Thatcher reflected, but again
he nodded comprehendingly. He wondered how much Tom's
various settlements cost him.

"Women are the devil," said the *bon vivant*, brooding into
his Martini. Then he brightened, "Still . . ."

"What do you have to do with *Fortinbras on Accounts
Receivable?*" Thatcher asked hastily. A widower himself, he
was prepared to sympathize with Tom's difficulties, but his
interest in the more active aspects of his social life was not
unlimited.

"Accounts receivable?" Robichaux repeated blankly. "What
are you talking about?"

"Tell me why I'm having lunch with you and with this
Clarence Fortinbras," Thatcher directed him. Tom was perfectly capable of starting at the beginning and going to the
end with reasonable competence; his mind, however, was
not the sort to permit shortcuts.

"Yes," he said. "Well, you know that Robichaux and
Devane have a big interest in National Calculating, don't
you?"

Thatcher nodded. "A big interest" meant that Tom's firm
held large amounts of National stock on their own account,
and occasionally used their inventory to firm the market, as
the euphemism went. They also acted as agent for customers
who wanted to buy or sell National Calculating stock, and
the dividing line between their functions was, at best, in an
ethical no-man's-land. Some brokerage houses sailed perilously close to the wind when they held a substantial "inter-

est," and Thatcher had always felt that touting a house-held stock to customers smacked of the trickster.

Robichaux and Devane was rightly proud of its unassailable rectitude in this precarious area.

"We haven't been able to sell any common stock to the Sloan," Robichaux said, diverted by a side grievance.

"It hasn't been doing very well lately, has it?" said Thatcher, trying to recall what he knew about National Calculating.

"Hell, no!" Robichaux exclaimed. "For the past two years they've been marking time. Then last year they skipped a dividend—and between the two of us, they're going to have to omit another one this year." He glared at a breadstick while Thatcher patiently waited for him to come to the point. He glanced at his watch: Fortinbras was scheduled to arrive in fifteen minutes, and he still knew nothing about Tom's reasons for this meeting.

"Come on, Tom," he said.

"They sell cash registers, you know, and those sales have held up pretty well. But during the war they expanded into computers, and that's where they're having trouble today. Their Commercial Sales aren't doing a thing; they sank five million dollars into it a couple of years ago, and it hasn't paid for itself. If it weren't for the cash registers and their government defense contracts, they'd be in a real hole." He looked up, recalled that he was talking to a potential customer, and added hastily, "They're basically sound . . ."

"Spare me, and get on with your story."

Robichaux assumed a look of exaggerated innocence. "Of course, I keep forgetting that we sold the Sloan some of their debentures a year or so ago . . ."

"What!" Thatcher exclaimed, genuinely surprised.

"Didn't you know that you took part of their bonds last year, John? About five thousand underlying shares . . ."

"I did not," Thatcher said crisply. "Just who did you gull?"

"Why, I think we sold them to Claster," Robichaux replied, his attention fixed on a portrait hanging over Thatcher's right shoulder.

"I see," Thatcher said grimly. Claster was head of the Investment Division, a doddering idiot, and scheduled to retire within the year.

". . . so I knew that the Sloan has an interest in this affair too," Robichaux was saying in elaborately reasonable tones.

Thatcher repressed the comment that rose to his lips.

"Just give me the facts, Tom," he said. "Who is this Clarence Fortinbras?"

"Fortinbras is a stockholder," said Robichaux. "He's got a bunch of stockholders together, and he's raising hell about one thing and another at National . . ."

"Just a minute. What does that mean?"

"Chip Mason—he's the president over there, you know—he tells me that Fortinbras and this bunch of stockholders have been bombarding them with letters. You know, whenever a corporation gets into trouble they start getting these crank letters. Well, Mason said they sent back the form letters, but this Fortinbras outfit turned out to be more persistent . . ."

"If he is *Fortinbras on Accounts Receivable*," said Thatcher somewhat acidly, "I don't think much of sending him a form letter. It might be wiser to listen to what he has to say." He looked at Robichaux with no affection.

"At any rate," Robichaux said, shrugging away the comment, "Mason says they were stunned to get a letter from something called . . . here, wait a minute." He fished a piece of paper from his pocket, affixed his glasses, and read, "The National Calculating Stockholders' Protest Committee." He took off his glasses, carefully put them away. "Mason says that this bunch is all nuts, and that they've been driving him crazy . . ."

"Forget Chip Mason," Thatcher said brutally. "Tell me why you're having lunch with Fortinbras if you're convinced that he's just a crank."

"I don't say he's a crank," protested Robichaux. "I'm just telling you what Chip . . . oh, all right," he said, as Thatcher glared. "Well, the other day this chap Fortinbras got in touch with Robichaux and Devane. I gather he wants us to join him in demanding some management changes. You know the sort of thing."

"It sounds like a good idea to me," Thatcher said unhelpfully.

"It puts us in a hell of a position," Robichaux said seriously. "On the one hand, we can't go around putting the skids under the boys at National Calculating; after all, we're their underwriters, and we can't get associated with dissident groups of cranks. It would give us a bad name. The corporations have to trust Robichaux and Devane."

"On the other hand . . ."

"On the other hand," he agreed, "we're none too happy with the earnings statement that National produced last month, and I don't think we're going to like next month's either. We're stuck with three hundred thousand shares, and we won't be able to sell them unless things start looking up. I want to hear what Fortinbras has to say. Mason says he's crazy . . ."

"Naturally Mason would," Thatcher said impatiently. "To a company president any stockholder who complains must be crazy . . ."

With a heavy, ruminative air Robichaux said, "I decided it wouldn't do any harm to talk to the man; if he's crazy, or a professional troublemaker, well, there's no harm done. But it might be useful to hear what he has to say . . ."

"And why am I here?"

"Because Robichaux and Devane needs an outside, impartial observer. Apart from your convertible debentures, you can't be expected to favor either National's management, or Fortinbras. And I don't want any misinterpretation about all of this."

Thatcher gave Robichaux's rather vaguely phrased statement his attention. To a business colleague, it was painfully clear: Robichaux and Devane—and worse luck, thanks to that muttonhead Claster, the Sloan Guaranty Trust—had an interest in what was happening at National Calculating.

But Robichaux and Devane, and for that matter the Sloan Guaranty Trust, could not consort with a professional cor-

porate gadfly or become involved in a nuisance suit. Among
other things, it would be a violation of the trust that companies reposed in them. And it would be bad for business.

So Robichaux, with a caution that seemed at variance with
his raffish appearance, was protecting himself with a third
party.

So much Thatcher understood. But, he thought, studying
Tom, who had returned to his drink, there was still a little
mystery here.

Tom Robichaux of Robichaux and Devane, banker to National Calculating, friend of President Charles Mason, would
be the last person in the world to be meeting Clarence Fortinbras at Fraunces Tavern under normal circumstances. With
or without John Thatcher.

He knew nothing about Fortinbras except what Mason
had told him. He did not even know that Fortinbras was a
well-known and respectable accountant. Yet here he was,
looking somewhat impatiently toward the doorway.

"Tom," Thatcher said carefully, "why are you having
lunch with this Fortinbras?"

"Why? I told you . . ."

"No, I mean why are you bothering with him? Did he
write you any details?"

"No," Robichaux replied unwillingly. "Just wrote to request a meeting about National Calculating. That's all."

"And you got all the rest of the information from the National people, didn't you?"

"Yes. Chip Mason asked me to talk to him, see if I could
head him off . . ."

Thatcher cut him short. "You wouldn't be running errands
for Chip Mason if you weren't interested in being here," he
said.

"Now, John," Robichaux blustered. "Naturally, we want to
head trouble off, if we can. I don't deny that personally I
am a little disappointed in National's performance; it isn't
what we had hoped for."

"Nonsense," retorted Thatcher. "You have a lot of companies whose performance isn't what you hoped for. What's
up, Tom? Why are you doing this for Mason?"

Robichaux rubbed his chin in a gesture of exasperation. "I'll be damned if I know," he said finally. "Mason asked me to talk to Fortinbras, and I said I would. But you're right, I've had a feeling . . . hell, I can't put it into words."

Thatcher leaned back and studied his companion. Feelings too vague to put into words, a sense of smell, the instinct of the trader—these are the things that make money on the Street.

And Tom Robichaux made money.

"I see," he said.

Robichaux looked alarmed; he was about to protest when a waiter hurried up.

"Mr. Robichaux's party?" he asked deferentially. "A Mr. Fortinbras."

# 2

# Enter Fortinbras

Thatcher and Robichaux rose as a small, spare, white-haired man of about seventy obeyed the waiter's beckoning finger, and made his way energetically toward their table. Mr. Fortinbras, Thatcher noticed, had the red, weather-beaten skin of the outdoorsman; he also boasted an untroubled air of self-assurance and excellent conservative tailoring. This is not a combination often encountered on Wall Street.

He identified himself crisply, acknowledged Robichaux's introductions, and then, as soon as they were all seated, plunged into the business at hand.

"I can guess what you're thinking," he said. "I know that Robichaux and Devane—and the Sloan Guaranty Trust—wouldn't touch the average stockholder group with a ten-foot pole. Cranks, corrupt lawyers, chiselers—that's what most of them are, and I know it. But I think that I can convince you that I—we—are a different thing altogether."

Thatcher could see that Robichaux was startled by Fortinbras's forthrightness.

"Er, yes. That is . . ."

"Now just how many of the facts . . . What? No, no thank you!" Fortinbras waved away the offer of a drink. "I don't want to waste your time. If you will tell me how much you know, I can go on from there. And answer any questions you want to raise."

He paused expectantly, surprising Robichaux, who had taken refuge in his drink, into a sputtering protest. Amused, Thatcher took pity on Tom, and resorted to diversionary tactics.

"Of course Robichaux and I have been disappointed in National Calculating's performance lately. I gather that you and some other stockholders aren't pleased with their current position."

This gentle trial balloon was instantly shot down.

"Yes, the Sloan bought some of their convertible debentures," Fortinbras responded, revealing that he knew more than at least one of the Sloan's vice presidents. "That surprised me, Thatcher. I thought you people had more sense." Fortinbras also had more brains than another of the Sloan's vice presidents, Thatcher thought ruefully. He reminded himself to have a little talk with Walter Bowman, chief of Research at the bank.

Fortinbras was continuing in a peppery voice, "We're not disappointed when our dividends are cut. We are suspicious!"

Robichaux emerged. "Suspicious of what?"

"Mismanagement, mistakes, covering up," said Fortinbras promptly.

"Oh, now look here," Robichaux began in a misguided attempt at cajolery. "I admit things haven't been going very well, but the latest financial statement . . ."

Fortinbras cut in. "National's last financial statement was a good bit of hocus-pocus. Not a bad job at all," he said, giving credit where credit was due. "But if you know where to look, it showed that only two divisions in the whole company are making money. Only two—Government Contracts and Table Models! And Table Models out in Elkhart is too small to matter much!" He leaned forward, fixed his very bright blue eyes on the unfortunate Robichaux, and said emphatically, "Every other division in the company is losing money!"

It was perfectly clear that he had not formed a high opinion of Robichaux's intelligence. "When only two divisions make money," he said slowly and distinctly, "I don't say that things aren't going well. I say that there's a crisis!"

Robichaux looked hopefully at his ally but John Thatcher assumed an expression of polite interest and remained unhelpfully silent. He attributed a large part of his success on Wall Street to the innate prudence that kept him from plunging into ill-advised controversy with men who had facts—and plenty of them, it seemed—at their fingertips.

Robichaux let reproach shine from his eyes for a moment, then rose to the demands of the moment by launching into a small discourse on the difficulties that could beset any rapidly growing company, on the growth potential at National Calculating, on defense industries in general. Despite Fortinbras's expression, he gained confidence as he went, reaching his conclusion just as the waiter, who had been making futile attempts to present Clarence Fortinbras with a menu, decided to act. He passed out the three cards, stationed himself directly by the table, poised his pencil, and coughed forcefully. Obediently the diners turned their attention to luncheon possibilities. Fortinbras scanned his menu, ordered lamb chops and a baked potato, then turned back to his hosts and politely waited for them to complete their selection. After a moment of thought, Thatcher ordered a crabmeat salad, then watched Robichaux suffer.

Because to Tom Robichaux, the proper choice of food and drink was a matter of importance. He would no more hurry through the planning of lunch than he would make a snap decision to underwrite a five-million-dollar issue. By nature a fusser, he added the enthusiasm of the gourmet to his natural instincts, making each order a stylized minuet of suggestion, rejection, and countersuggestion.

But he was not immune to atmosphere. As his detailed inquiries into the construction of the salad dressing protracted themselves, Fortinbras, while remaining perfectly motionless and silent, communicated enough restrained impatience to unnerve him—and to convince John Thatcher that attempting to introduce small talk into the interval was futile. Small talk was clearly not part of Clarence Fortinbras's social armory.

At last Robichaux dithered himself into petulant repudiation of all suggestion. The waiter played his final card. There was an offer of olive oil and vinegar. Perhaps the gentleman would care to mix his own. The gentleman would. The waiter retired with the triumphant air of one who has handled a difficult situation well.

Unfortunately, Fortinbras had not forgotten Tom's speech.

"Mr. Robichaux," he said, "if I may say so, you are talking complete nonsense. National Calculating has had five years of low profits—the lowest in the industry, for that matter!—despite the fact that they are the only company that makes Target Control Releases for the Army. And their earnings are still sinking." He eyed Robichaux severely. "I intend to do something about it!"

Thatcher, for one, believed him. While in general he was inclined to be skeptical about strong claims of this nature, he had the feeling that if Clarence Fortinbras were determined to do something, then something would be done. The question, however, was what action Fortinbras (of *Fortinbras on Accounts Receivable*) would consider appropriate.

Even Tom Robichaux, who made a career out of imperturbability, was shaken. "What do you intend to do?" he asked apprehensively.

Fortinbras paused—for dramatic effect, Thatcher was tempted to think, although it might have been to collect his thoughts—then said with ominous quiet: "I intend to inspect the books of National Calculating. I shall examine their financial records with a fine-tooth comb. And I will find out what they are covering up—what they are concealing from their stockholders!"

"Oh," said Robichaux weakly. It might have been a groan.

"And I hope that I'll have the support of the Sloan Guaranty Trust and Robichaux and Devane," Fortinbras added. He then applied himself to his lamb chops.

Despite a congenital disinclination to hurl himself into meat choppers, John Thatcher was tempted.

"Exactly how do you intend to get access to the books at

National Calculating?" he inquired. Robichaux, he could see, was afraid to ask.

Fortinbras looked up with a wintry smile. "I am going to make a formal request of the president, Charles Mason . . ."

Robichaux uttered a strangled noise, and Fortinbras glanced indulgently at his flushed countenance. "I know what you're going to say," he said. "He won't cooperate." He considered Mason for a moment, then added, "Now that man's a nincompoop."

Amused, Thatcher watched Robichaux turn an unlovelier red, then said to Fortinbras, "Am I correct in assuming that you want us to join you in trying to convince Mason to let you inspect National's books?"

"It would make things easier," Fortinbras agreed. Thatcher heard nothing in his voice to indicate that he was not willing to do things the hard way. "Look at it this way, Thatcher. We have reasonable grounds for the request—there's an appalling mess at National. And I am not only a stockholder, and representative of a substantial number of other dissatisfied stockholders—I am a well-known accountant. If Mason cooperates, we can make our investigations without bad publicity . . ."

"Publicity!" Robichaux grasped at this straw. "Good Lord, man, have you thought of what this will do to the price of the stock?"

Thatcher ignored this. Fortinbras's tone had left no doubt in his mind that he had an alternative plan.

"And if the Sloan and Robichaux and Devane don't join you? What are you planning to do?"

Fortinbras looked at him. "I'll get a court order," he said.

This goaded Robichaux into another foray from behind the battery of shakers and cruets. "You wouldn't want to do that. Think of the market . . ."

"I would regret doing it," said Fortinbras, who did not sound particularly regretful. "Getting a court order is the worst possible way to do things. But if Mason makes it necessary, then I will! I would welcome your help—just as I would welcome signs of intelligence from Mason—but let me make this point clear: I am convinced that the management at National Calculating is obstructionist either from massive stupidity, a desire to conceal some colossal ineptitude—or something worse!"

He was not, Thatcher noted, alarmed or surprised by the situation he postulated. Stupidity and ineptitude were not rarities in Clarence Fortinbras's world, whatever that world was. Thatcher wished he had more information about the man; presumably, if that expensive tailoring were any guide, he had done something beside write a textbook with a ridiculous name.

He was continuing calmly. "That's why I want to know if Robichaux and Devane or the Sloan Guaranty Trust will support me."

Robichaux, at best not a rapid thinker, simply goggled at him. Thatcher replied with the honesty that he felt the accountant deserved.

"The Sloan can't touch it, Fortinbras," he said quietly. "In the first place, we're bond holders . . ."

"Yes, that puts you in a different position," said Fortinbras in a friendly voice. "I appreciate that."

". . . and under no circumstances could we become involved with dissident groups of stockholders—no matter how distinguished."

Fortinbras acknowledged the compliment with a nod. "That's what I expected, Thatcher. Perfectly sensible attitude. Now, Mr. Robichaux?"

Robichaux started visibly, then, looking distraught, launched into another disjointed peroration, featuring such phrases as "respect of the financial community . . . privileged relationship . . . moving slowly and quietly . . ."

"And you're a friend of Mason, aren't you?" said Fortinbras mildly.

"I can assure you that I would never let such considerations influence my judgment," Robichaux replied with dignity.

Fortinbras was unimpressed. He surveyed his companions with what looked remarkably like relief. "I was expecting this response, you know," he said rather jauntily. "In a way, I'm glad. Working with big institutions—you'll forgive my saying so, won't you?—might cramp my style. I'm a lone wolf—and I really want to get my teeth into this thing." He gave a wolfish bark of laughter that boded ill for National Calculating, and went on, "And then, I'm afraid you might slow me down. I have a tight time schedule."

"Time schedule?" Thatcher asked.

Fortinbras gave him a look that was almost conspiratorial. "Mason has given me an appointment this afternoon. If you don't mind, I think that I'll skip dessert and coffee and get over to National Calculating. Then, after Mason has made a fool of himself, I'll have time to see my lawyer. We can file for a court order within the week."

No more than five minutes later, Fortinbras vigorously shook hands wtih his hosts and hurried away.

Robichaux sank back into his chair. "Court order! Do you think Mason can talk him out of it?"

Thatcher was feeling invigorated by his exposure to Fortinbras. He laughed aloud. "Tom, Mason can't talk a dog into barking!"

Robichaux ignored this. "I wonder what we can do to head that nut off," he muttered.

Unsympathetically, Thatcher stirred his coffee. "Take my word for it, a Sherman tank couldn't stop Clarence Fortinbras."

Robichaux drummed fingers on the table. "I wonder how much stock he represents. You know, John, I wouldn't be surprised if this turns out to mean real trouble for National . . ." He broke off. "And what in hell is funny about that?"

"I just like your lightning deductions," Thatcher replied.

Robichaux was in no mood for pleasantries. "I wasn't happy at the way he talked about National Calculating. He sounded pretty convinced—about something."

"Yes?" said Thatcher encouragingly.

Robichaux brooded for a moment, then faced the music. "What," he reluctantly asked, "what do you suppose he could turn up? Chip is straight as a die . . . and anyway, he isn't up to pulling off anything fancy."

"Fortinbras will turn up everything that there is to turn up," Thatcher predicted equably. "Every idiocy that your friend Chip Mason has perpetrated—and as I recall Mason, that will be a considerable number. And Mason will certainly provoke enough hostility in their conference today to rouse Fortinbras to a fever pitch."

Robichaux then justified Thatcher's description of him as a man of almost inspired simplicity.

"I don't like it."

Thatcher cocked an eyebrow at him. "I don't like it myself. The Sloan is going to lose money, I suspect. And you are going to lose money. Nevertheless, let's retain our famous balance and order dessert. You have to admit that Fortinbras was refreshing in his way."

"First Dorothy—and I'll admit that I'm a little worried about that, John—then this!" Robichaux grumbled after he had ordered his apple pie. "Frankly, it's getting me down."

His exercise in self-pity elicited nothing but brutal candor from Thatcher. "I don't feel sorry for you, Tom," he said. "Just think of those poor fish over at National. We're going to lose money—no, I don't like it either, but we'll survive—but Mason and the rest of them are going to be blasted into smithereens. And they won't know what's hit them until it's too late!"

# 3

# The Company and Fortinbras

Thatcher's sympathy was not misplaced. At just about the time that he and Tom Robichaux were finishing their excellent coffee and preparing to return to work, the advance winds of the great Fortinbras storm were reaching National Calculating's executive offices in the Southern Bourbon Building. As Mary Sullivan could have told him, if they weren't dangerous in themselves, they were extremely menacing.

Miss Sullivan, as befits the competent secretary—and because she was interested in such things—had charted the course of the disturbance as it approached.

At ten o'clock that morning, she had circulated Mr. Mason's memo to the Division Managers: a meeting at two-thirty with Mr. Clarence Fortinbras who had already been in correspondence with them.

"Another meeting?" asked Dr. Richter (Research and Development). Dr. Richter was young, blond, and somewhat bull-necked; he asked the question with what he thought was an irresistible smile.

"That's what it says," she answered sweetly.

Mr. Blaney (Commercial Sales) was hearty. "What's up this time, Mary?" he shouted, rapidly scanning the document she handed him. "Uh-huh, Fortinbras, I see." Harry Blaney who was not so young, had a round face, a thin thatch of brown hair, and normally a guileless, if heavily tanned, countenance. But as she watched him, she saw his cheeriness collapse when he noticed Allen Hammond's name on the circulation list. Allen Hammond was the assistant division manager of Commercial Sales; he was also the president's nephew learning the business, as the saying goes. These things are never easy.

"I'll put it on Mr. Rutledge's desk," Clara Floyd in Government Contracts promised. "He's in New Jersey until lunch. Are they in a flap up there?"

"You know how they are, Clara," Mary replied.

She returned to her elegant quarters just outside the president's office and applied herself to her work, which included a long memorandum to Table Model Division (Elkhart, Indiana) about a new union contract, and an equally long—but livelier—memorandum to the Empire Club about the Reunion Dinner "for Harvard's football greats in the New York City area."

"It's going to be a great evening, Miss Sullivan," said Mr. Mason when he strolled out a few minutes later to see how things were coming. Mr. Mason was a big soft-looking man with a troubled pink face.

"We've got forty responses already, Mr. Mason," she replied, because she was a kind-hearted girl.

". . . and old Bull Peabody is coming up from Washington," he said, genuine enthusiasm lighting his faded blue eyes. Bull and Chip Mason, as Mary Sullivan knew all too well, had been the famous Twin Battering Rams of the great 1929 Harvard team. Before she fully grasped the depth of Mr. Mason's lack of interest in cash registers and computers, she had unwisely told him about her brother Jack, a tackle with the Chicago Bears, a fact that led him to infer sympathy with his heroic past.

"Did I ever tell you . . ."

"I put the Fortinbras correspondence in this folder for you," she cut in ruthlessly.

"Oh, yes," Chip Mason said, eying it with distaste. "I suppose I'd better look it over."

She turned suggestively to her typewriter, and he wandered back into his office, possibly to look at the folder. By the second month of her employment, Mary Sullivan had discovered that despite his many shortcomings the president of National Calculating took direction. Possibly coaching was a better word.

Bad as things were, they would have been far worse had it not been for that fact.

Promptly at two-thirty, Clarence Fortinbras presented himself at Mary Sullivan's desk.

"I think Mr. Mason is expecting me," he said with a marked New England accent.

Knowing her chief's capacity for self-delusion, Mary doubted it, but she said, "This way, Mr. Fortinbras," and led him into the president's office. Before she shut the door behind him, she saw that the Battering Ram looked apprehensive as he rose to greet his visitor, and that Dr. Richter was the only Division Manager not yet present.

He strode in twenty minutes later, pushing a hand through his crew cut. "Couldn't get away," he said importantly.

"I believe they're waiting for you, Dr. Richter," she pointed out when he showed a tendency to stop and discuss the demands on his valuable time.

"Oh, yes," he said and disappeared into the president's office.

Thereafter, Mary Sullivan worked without further executive interruption, solving several small problems which could be expected to throw Mason into a welter of indecision, and sending some intelligent directives to Elkhart. At three o'clock she bore Mr. Mason's glass of milk into the room, her practiced eye noting that Clarence Fortinbras retained the slightly rugged air of calm that had distinguished him when he greeted her, but that Mason and the senior staff looked, according to their temperaments, ruffled, angry, disdainful, or mulish. Dr. Richter was trying to look profound. Allen Hammond smiled at her.

At four o'clock, the mumble of voices stopped, the door opened, and a red-faced Mason escorted Fortinbras through the office. Fortinbras murmured a courteous word of fare-well, nodded to Miss Sullivan, and left. She waited for the rest of the staff to eddy out, and back to their appointed places. Instead Mason silently returned to his office, shut the door, and the steady rumble of voices was resumed.

That was when Mary Sullivan knew that something was up.

"Well!" said Allen Hammond in amused tones.

"What does that mean?" Mason demanded pettishly as he returned to the chair at the head of the long table. Hammond, a thorn in Harry Blaney's flesh because he was the president's nephew, was an irritant to his uncle because of his status as Founder's Grandson. He was a pleasantly ugly, intelligent young man whose presence never failed to remind Chip that the entire Mason family agreed that the president wasn't half the man his father had been.

"It means that that was quite a session," Allen Hammond said equably. "He's impressive, isn't he?"

"He's a nuisance, that's what he is!" Mason said fretfully. Instinctively he looked around the table for support. Harry Blaney was staring glumly at a scratch pad; Morris Richter had assumed a judicious look, and was gazing abstractedly into the distance. Allen Hammond looked intelligent and respectful, which was no balm to his uncle. Only Jay Rutledge, his creased homely face as expressionless as ever, responded.

"Well, now, Chip," he said, a hint of his native Georgia in his voice, "He is a troublesome little man"—Rutledge was six feet tall—"but I think we took the right line with him. We can't tolerate fishing expeditions into the books every time anybody gets a bee in his bonnet . . ."

"I tell you, he isn't 'anybody,'" Blaney said for the second time. "He's *Fortinbras on Accounts Receivable*. He's an authority in the field of corporate accounting, he taught for twenty years at Maine, and he's the one who single-handed got the boys at New England Marine to give up that depreciation system of theirs!"

Mason felt the familiar stab of pain in his stomach. It had

been a long meeting, and he could not delude himself that he had handled it very well. His every overture had been refused with cold indifference.

"Call me Chip!" he had said.

Fortinbras had looked at him. "Mr. Mason," he replied, "I want to be sure that we understand each other."

Well, they understood each other, he thought as he chewed on a Gelusil. Not that he had been able to present the company's case well; Fortinbras's calm refutation of his host's comments and his unexpectedly detailed knowledge had rattled Mason.

"How was I to know that he knew all that?" he demanded, stung by the injustice of the whole thing.

Harry Blaney was tactless enough to tell him. "I don't know why you didn't check up on him, Chip," he said, earnestly helpful "I called Berman this morning, and he put me onto the comptroller at New England Marine. It only took two phone calls to find out who he was, and to be honest with you, I think we've made a mistake with him."

It was obvious to everybody at the table that National Calculating had erred with Clarence Fortinbras. Nevertheless, Chip Mason thought resentfully, he disliked people who went around being honest. Of course, Blaney was a Business School type if there ever was one—not the same thing as a Harvard man, God knows!—and Mason endured his heavy-handed, jolting geniality on the theory that it was good for business. Quite early in life, Charles Mason had been brought to see that he lacked the hard-hitting vigor that would push cash registers to the top, and he was resigned to dynamic subordinates. But Blaney seemed to possess the defects of the go-getter with none of his virtues: his division, Commercial Sales, was going into the red again this month.

". . . why does he want to examine the books?" Richter broke the silence by asking. His brilliant scientific abilities kept him involved with research projects and development techniques but, although totally innocent of any business knowledge, he liked to ask penetrating questions. The affectation was harmless enough except when, as now, it required an answer.

"He wants to see the books," said Blaney as one talking to an idiot, "because we've done so damn badly last year and this year that he thinks we're guilty of mismanagement. Or worse. You heard him, didn't you? 'We may find something suggestive.'" He threw down a pencil in disgust.

"Well, now," Jay Rutledge said ruminatively. "I think you're letting him get under your skin. Can't say that I blame you, mind you. I never saw a man so sure of himself. Still, when you run into a little trouble, you have to expect something of the sort. Remember David Paul, Chip? Back in '48? Now this Fortinbras is a different sort, I grant you, but I think we can handle him."

This was a long speech for Rutledge, and Mason was grateful for it. Blaney too looked grateful, if slightly surprised.

Because Rutledge's division—Government Contracts—was the only division in the company that consistently made money. The Target Control Release which Rutledge had developed was a small computer ideally suited for light artillery work. National Calculating was the only company to manufacture it and, in turn, the TCR brought National Calculating almost all its profits.

Normally Jay Rutledge, by nature unforthcoming, was isolated from his colleagues because he was involved with neither their problems nor their disappointments. He spent most of his time in his own division's New Jersey plant; if Morris Richter and Harry Blaney resented his independence, they were not in a position to complain about it.

He tamped his pipe and looked up. "Well?" he asked with a slight smile at the unanimous relief his words brought.

"I'm damned glad you're taking that attitude, Jay," Blaney said bluntly. "I'm not always sure where you stand when something like this comes up. I like to think that we're all on the same team, and I'm glad that you think of it that way too."

"I don't know what you mean, Harry," Rutledge said calmly, "I'm not a great one for meetings and long talks, but I agree that we can't just hand over the prerogatives of management to anybody who comes around. Whether it's the unions or Mr. Clarence Fortinbras. So long as I'm the head of Government Contracts, he doesn't set foot in it."

"I knew we could rely on you," Mason said. National Calculating might have its troubles, he thought, brightening slightly, but it was game. A second thought exploded the bubble. "What about that court order he was talking about?" he said anxiously. "Do you think he's got a chance of getting one?"

A depressed silence ensued.

"He'd have to show cause," Hammond said at last, in an unsuitably light voice. "That means he'd have to satisfy the court that this was more than"—he bobbed his head to Rutledge, who had fallen into his normal Lincolnesque posture of deep thought—"more than a fishing expedition."

"Can he do it?" asked Richter, still pursuing the truth regardless of its implications.

"What do you mean by that?" Mason cried.

"Now, Chip, don't get excited," Rutledge intervened calmly, the southern note in his voice deepening. "I don't think there's much likelihood of it," he said to Richter. "And if he does, we won't have anything to hide."

"He won't want to look at the books of Government Contracts," Blaney said gloomily. "He'll be in my hair, wanting to know why we're carrying the kind of inventory we're carrying, why our distribution costs are so high . . ." He broke off, looked at Richter with dislike and added, "Then he'll be after you!"

The scientist was startled out of a narcissistic examination of his hands. "Me!"

"Sure. He'll want to know why we spent $156,000 on that bright idea of yours for a diode casing, and then had to scrap it . . ."

"You can't plan scientific work like an assembly line," Richter retorted. "You don't know ahead of time what will pan out and what won't."

"I'm not saying you can," Blaney replied. "I'm just saying that we're the ones who'll have to put up with this prying old fool. If he gets a court order—which I hope to God he doesn't."

"You know," Allen Hammond said without malice, "after today's conference, I don't know that I'd agree with you, Harry. I think he's going to be gunning for all of us."

They instinctively turned to Rutledge who smiled, a trifle grimly. "He sure put my back up," he agreed, "and I think you're right. If he gets a court order, he'll be all over the place. But without one, he's not setting foot in the door of my division."

"That's the spirit," Blaney said, trying to shake his edginess. "Well, I guess we'd better get back to work. Was there anything else, Chip?"

Mason, recalled from some private reverie, frowned at the regrettable lack of deference in Blaney's voice.

"I don't think so," he said, trying to muster some heartiness of his own. "Unless you want to report on that new cutting process you were talking about last month . . ."

Hammond permitted himself a small smile while Richter assumed a spuriously expectant attitude.

"We've had some trouble in the plant with it," Blaney said in a careful show of candor. "I still think it's going to work out," he added with a defiant look at Richter, "but it's a little tricky."

Hammond and Richter had both opposed the new process.

". . . so, we're going to work on it some more, and see if we can straighten out the bugs. Otherwise, it won't do us any good . . ."

"As well as costing us forty-seven thousand for the new tools," Mason said fretfully. "Jay, what do you think about this?"

"Leave me out, Chip," he said without bothering to remove the pipe from his mouth. "Harry sounded pretty sensible to me when he talked about it, and he's running the tests. He's the one who knows whether it's going to work or not."

"Have you tried anything like it on the TCR's?" asked Blaney.

"No," Rutledge replied. "We have to stick with the original specifications we gave to the Army. Any change would have to be okayed by General Cartwright and the Ordnance people."

"The reason it's worth trying," said Blaney, who tended to repetition, "is that we can't sell at a profitable price unless we find some way to cut costs. Remember, on our commercial sales we just sell the computer itself, not the whole TCR . . ."

"Yes, yes," Mason said. "Selling just components is a different proposition. But it's funny that we can make the same sort of thing in two divisions and only show a profit from one." He sounded depressed.

"It is," Blaney said in an aggrieved voice.

"Well, we'll hope for the best," Mason said optimistically.

He did not specify the area.

# 4

# In the Wings

On the bad-penny principle that governs human affairs, John Putnam Thatcher found that National Calculating Corporation, about which he had rarely if ever thought before his luncheon with Robichaux and Fortinbras, was now popping up wherever he looked.

In some areas, of course, this was to be expected. Upon his return from Fraunces Tavern, he had immediately summoned Walter Bowman, his Chief of Research, into conference. What he learned about National Calculating—and the Sloan's investment in its convertible debentures—made painful listening.

"God knows what got into Claster," Bowman summarized. "Maybe he knows something that we don't." Since both he and Thatcher knew Claster and his work, his voice lacked conviction.

"I'd better talk to him about it," said Thatcher unenthusiastically. But it was a week before he steeled himself to confront Burton Claster, head of the Investment Division. Claster was being tactfully but firmly nudged to retirement by a Board out of patience with similar ventures; he was determinedly resisting these moves with a series of clumsy attempts to cover his errors, enlist allies, and justify his existence. A conference with him was not undertaken lightly these days.

Nevertheless, it took place. Emerging, Thatcher summed

up what he had learned: the situation at National Calculating was, if anything, worse than Clarence Fortinbras had
suggested. More germane, the situation in the Investment
Division of the Sloan Guaranty Trust was worse than the
Board of Directors guessed. Thatcher was going to have to
deal with the latter; he hoped that he had washed his hands
of the former.

This hope was in vain. Not three days later, Walter Bowman called his attention to a discreet paragraph in the *Journal of Commerce.*

"So he got his court order," Thatcher mused aloud. He
had never doubted for a moment that Clarence Fortinbras
would.

"National didn't have a leg to stand on," said Bowman,
levering his great bulk out of the chair. "If it had been anybody else, maybe—but not Fortinbras."

Thatcher looked at him. It should have occurred to him
that the omniscient Bowman was the man to know precisely
who Clarence Fortinbras was. Bowman did indeed. Falling
back into his chair, he obliged Thatcher with a brief description. Clarence Fortinbras was an accountant's accountant. When Price, Waterhouse was reduced to wringing its
hands in despair, Fortinbras was the man to be called in.
If the problems raised by a major auto firm's going public
proved very delicate, then a quiet feeler would go forth
from the independent auditors—to Clarence Fortinbras.
Never bothering to acquire a clientele of his own, Fortinbras
had been content to let his brethren seek him out. Firmly
maintaining his residence and his appointment at the University of Maine until his retirement, he had carefully nur-
tured a reputation for expertise and eccentricity.

". . . and he's made a fortune, too. Why, that textbook
alone—*Fortinbras on Accounts Receivable*—that's the accountant's Dr. Spock!"

Thatcher digested this.

"He'll be raising hell at National Calculating," Bowman
said cheerfully in parting.

"And enjoying it thoroughly," Thatcher replied.

"That," said Bowman, "just makes it worse."

Both of them were right. Armed with his court order, Clarence Fortinbras speedily set about raising hell at the Southern Bourbon Building, and enjoying himself in the process. Thoughtfully, for he was a thoughtful man, he informed his wife of both developments as soon as he could.

"Emily," he said crisply into the mouthpiece, "I just want to warn you that I'm going to be late for dinner tonight. I have to get settled here and organize things . . ."

From Connecticut, Emily's voice spoke rather sadly about a roast with Yorkshire pudding. It lacked authority; thirty years of marriage had left their mark on Emily.

". . . problems with deferred charges, just as I suspected," Clarence said happily.

"How nice," said Emily. "Tell me, Clarence, did they give you a nice office?"

Clarence loosed a bray of laughter. "Stuck me in a closet," he said without rancor. "Mason and the rest of them are burned up. But I told them that I was ready to go to court again if it's necessary, so I've got an assistant. And I'll get more . . ."

"That's nice," said Emily vaguely. "Clarence, I do hope you're not going to make a lot of trouble down there, particularly for Margaret . . ."

Clarence did not share his wife's high opinion of peace and quiet.

"I'm not making trouble, Emily, I'm finding it!" he said firmly. "Well, I'd better get to work. Mark my words, before the day is out, National Calculating is going to realize that I mean business!"

"Oh, dear," said Emily.

Clarence Fortinbras made his boast on Monday and possibly one day was too ambitious a forecast. Novel perceptions were not readily assimilated at National Calculating Corporation. But certainly, by the end of that week, nobody had the slightest doubt that he meant business. His relations with Charles Mason, discordant from the start, deteriorated under the impact of day-to-day contact. The president of National, nettled by what he regarded as an intransigent lack of cooperation by the Supreme Court of the State of New York, undertook misguided skirmishes designed to restrict Fortinbras's activities. Fortinbras reacted to these guerrilla tactics in precisely the manner John Thatcher had predicted —by digging in his heels, laying back his ears, and becoming less controllable than ever. He flourished his court order, at one point produced his attorney, and threatened contempt proceedings. The resultant fireworks achieved so much entertainment value that, in the words of one lowly employee, you hated to go home for fear of what you might miss. By Wednesday the mail room was making book on the outcome. But after a notable early victory centering on access to the executive men's room, Chip Mason lost ground steadily. Fortinbras successfully maintained his right to enter the premises, to make extracts and photostats, to plunge into files at will and to communicate his findings to fellow shareholders.

By Friday, Mason retired from the arena, a broken man. No further attempt was made to restrain Fortinbras, and he was left to enjoy the fruits of his court order (and the freedom of the public men's room) as best he could.

With the front office wrapped in an impenetrable cloud of lordly indifference, National's intelligence network fell back on a resource natural in time of crisis. Rumors flowed unchecked. Fortinbras was to be the next president, and Charles Mason was on the way out; Fortinbras was the agent of a take-over group, and a merger would be announced any day; Fortinbras was the advance guard of a full-scale Congressional investigation. Most of the clerical staff remained in genuine confusion about the source of Fortinbras's authority, a confusion he made no effort to dispel.

Fortinbras was not slow to consolidate his position. By the simple method of approaching various menials and crisply barking orders, he was soon absorbing the full-time energies of one secretary, two comptometer operators, and three messenger boys, who did nothing but rush from office to office, collecting files to add to the growing heap which was rapidly creating a first-class fire hazard in the cubicle from which Fortinbras was directing all this frenetic activity. Empires are not built without inconveniencing somebody. In this case the nominal employer of the secretary was sacrificed to the tide of progress. His complaints to the office manager were unavailing. Miss Quackenbush, who had never surmounted the problems inherent in reordering office supplies, was already paralyzed by the raid on her comptometer staff. The chief of the Messenger Service was no longer on speaking terms with anyone in the Accounting Department. Harassed telegrams flowed to Elkhart, Indiana, where the controller of National Calculating, being no fool, immediately extended his absence from the home office. No controller likes to see his financial records in hostile hands: Harrison decided to spare himself that painful sight.

Only one person was stirred professionally by the descent of Clarence Fortinbras. Stanley Draper, junior accountant, had held a lonely and unenviable position at National during the four months which had elapsed since his graduation from Cornell. Debarred alike from association with the book-keepers by virtue of his college degree in accounting and from association with the assistant controllers by his lack of standing as a certified public accountant, he had led an isolated and often uncomfortable existence. His only formal colleague was a man some thirty years older than himself who had started with National in 1929 as a bookkeeper, and raised himself to the level of accountant by thirteen years' assiduous attendance at night school. Not unnaturally exhausted by this sustained effort, he had decided to rest on his laurels. But Stanley was young, and his ambitions assumed a less negative character. He yearned after the world of big business. Not the world of Expense Accounts and Petty Cash which were his chief professional concerns at the moment, but the world of mergers and poolings of interest, of write-ups and write-downs, of depreciation and reserves. In other words, Stanley Draper wanted to be a very important man. Like Clarence Fortinbras.

One of the last to hear news on the company grapevine, Stanely Draper had received no warning of Fortinbras's arrival. He entered his office the day after this event to find the following masterful memo awaiting him.

To: STANLEY P. DRAPER
From: CLARENCE FORTINBRAS

Date: October 17
Subject: Internal Audit

By virtue of the authority vested in me under a Court Order
issued October 13 by the Supreme Court of New York, I am
undertaking a complete examination of the Company's records and financial accounts. You are requested to report to
me at 2:00 this afternoon for instructions concerning assistance to be rendered by your department.

Stanley was delighted. He would no more have questioned
the authority of Clarence Fortinbras to press him into service
than he would have questioned the summons of his local
draft board.

Stanley Draper presented himself promptly at the appointed hour with the most cooperative face Fortinbras had
yet encountered at National Calculating. The great accountant was not slow to capitalize on his advantage. For three
days Stanley Draper, to his complete satisfaction, received
calls from the adjoining office with increasing frequency. On
the third day Fortinbras swept him up at noontime, carried
him off to lunch at L'Aiglon, and for two hours regaled him
with an animated description of the opportunities open to
a bright young man in accounting. From that moment, Stanley was Clarence Fortinbras's devoted acolyte. The Accounting Department became hardened to the sight of Stanley
rushing back and forth between the two offices, of Stanley
closeted with Fortinbras for hours, of Stanley busily com-
piling lists, checking files, and importantly sending the office
boy out for sandwiches so that he and Fortinbras could improve the lunch hour by organizing and assessing the task
before them. It was the middle of the month and, as far as
Stanley was concerned, those duties in connection with Expense Accounts and Petty Cash for which he was employed
(and paid) could be deferred until the monthly closing. In
the meantime, he was prepared to sit at his mentor's feet and
imbibe wisdom.

"Always check discrepancies. They have no place in good accounts."

"It's your sense of smell that counts, Stanley. Train it first, then trust it."

"Small jobs can be done just as well as large ones. Everybody has brains enough to know that you should be very careful with ten-million deals."

"So long as there's a paper record at all, you can track things down. The only really successful frauds have been the ones that nobody tried to substantiate."

These private tutorials were a genuine source of inspiration to Stanley, while Clarence Fortinbras accepted his transparent adulation indulgently. He was used to students, and sometimes missed them. Nevertheless, a steady diet of Stanley Draper was a little too rich for his aging blood, and he was relieved to see his calendar, on the morning of Monday, October 23, warn him that a meeting of the National Calculating Stockholders' Protest Committee was scheduled that afternoon.

"Good, good," Fortinbras said to himself. Regina Plout was perfectly acceptable as a change from young Draper, if from no other point of view. Every cloud has its silver lining. Pausing at Stanley Draper's office to inform him that he would be absent for the rest of the day, Fortinbras headed for the elevator with a jaunty step. How right he had been to stay away from formal business life. Exchanging a curt nod with Charles Mason, who shared his elevator, he decided that office life might be the death of him.

He was right.

# 5

# *Fortinbras and the Conspirators*

No one could deny that Regina Plout's living room on Central Park West provided a wholehearted contrast to the interior decor of National Calculating's accounting department. For years she had been a part-time enthusiast of home decorating and a faithful reader of *Better Homes and Gardens*. But the death of Samuel Plout, the very substantial price which his partnership interest in Lady Godiva Foundation Garments, Incorporated, had commanded, and the removal for reasons best known to themselves of Mr. and Mrs. Samuel Plout, Jr., to one of the more inaccessible points on Long Island had all conspired to transform a mild hobby into an all-consuming interest. When *House Beautiful* heralded the return to elegance, she had been one of the first to lend a sympathetic ear. Louis Quinze was the style favored by Mrs. Plout, and she was fond of saying that she, personally, saw nothing wrong with ornateness provided it was expensive enough. Various decorators had been happy to take her at her word, and two years of hard spending had gone into producing the swagged draperies, the polished parquet floors, and the slim, uncomfortable side chairs which now housed the third meeting of the National Calculating Stockholders' Protest Committee.

Indeed, Mrs. Plout's membership in this group stemmed

directly from the finished perfection of her home. Left without an occupation, and enraged by a cut in her dividends, she had responded to Clarence Fortinbras's circular letter as to a clarion call. Her very sizable holdings not only made her a welcome addition to the group—they lent some substance to Fortinbras's appearance in court as the representative of a substantial stockholder element. Her personal qualities, which did not include tact, consideration, or intelligence, could never have recommended her even to a Protest Committee, but Mrs. Plout had one valuable characteristic: she was not idle. She brought bustling vigor to the business of writing, telephoning, soliciting funds, addressing envelopes, consulting with the printer, and finding out about third-class mail. And while Fortinbras was sorely tried by her habit of insisting that every meeting of more than three people be conducted in accordance with *Robert's Rules of Order,* he had to admit that the pompous solemnity with which these tactics endowed their proceedings was thoroughly enjoyed by most of the participants. It was inevitable that Regina Plout should be elected secretary-treasurer by popular acclaim. Listening to her reports, thought Fortinbras, was a small price to pay for having all the work done.

". . . three hundred and seventy-six dollars for postage, two hundred and fifty-two dollars for stationery, and three hundred and eighteen dollars for printing, coming to a grand total of twelve hundred and thirty-two dollars. We didn't have to include a typist's fee due to the fine help of Mrs. Evelyn Harries and Mrs. Miriam Dennis who addressed all the envelopes. I think we should have a motion for a vote of thanks to show our gratitude to these two ladies for all their work."

She paused to look about her expectantly. Fortinbras scowled at a Fragonard print across the room, and the danger passed. A retired doctor made the motion; it was duly seconded and carried to the accompaniment of blushing disclaimers by the two elderly widows involved, suitable expressions of gratification by most of those present, and a look of absolute disgust from a wealthy and unemployed young man who had come to the meeting because his trustee

had told him that he should take an interest in his investments. Mrs. Plout surveyed the scene indulgently for a moment before continuing.

"Now you mustn't think that we've just been wasting the
Committee's money. Some of you may feel that over a thousand dollars is a lot to spend on circularizing. But the results
of our mailing have now been calculated, and I'm proud to
announce that more than 30 percent of the stockholders responded favorably. We now represent over 14 percent of the
outstanding stock."

There was a stir of approval from the twelve people listening. One woman (who was there in the face of her husband's
heated objections) nodded complacently to herself. That
would teach Arthur to say he had only put the shares in her
name for tax purposes! The second doctor present took out
a notebook and made an entry. Mrs. Dennis and Mrs. Harries
looked modestly pleased.

Mrs. Plout hesitated for a moment, as if reluctant to come
to the inevitable moment when she must yield the sweets of
public speaking to a successor. She consulted the index cards
fanned out before her, made a great show of ticking off
points, shook her head momentously, and finally succumbed
to the temptation of revenging herself on the next speaker
with a lengthy introduction.

"Mr. Clarence Fortinbras needs no introduction to us . . .
first raised the possibility of organizing ourselves . . . enthusiasm and devotion . . . an inspiration to us all . . . will
report to us on his findings . . . Mr. Clarence Fortinbras!"

The company settled down expectantly for the *pièce de
résistance* of the meeting. In response to Regina Plout's busy
directions, Fortinbras obediently proceeded to the small
table serving as a rostrum, paused for a moment while he
collected the attention of the gathering in a practiced manner, and then briskly squared away to the business of de-
livering his report. After dealing faithfully with the petty
harassments of his first few days at National and allowing
himself a fruity chuckle at the nature of the sanitary facilities provided for his accommodation, he produced a copy of
National's Annual Report to its stockholders, and flipped

expertly to the financial statements. There was a subdued bustle as eleven people searched for similar documents in handbags, briefcases, and down between the sofa cushions. The rich young man had failed to bring his copy. Regina Plout hissed at him sharply. He shied nervously, and she ostentatiously tiptoed to an elegant sideboard in which she maintained a supply while Fortinbras courteously suspended his speech. The young man accepted his material ungraciously, permitted his hostess to find his place, and Fortinbras continued.

Rapidly reviewing what he regarded as the weak spots in the financial summaries, he was brought to an early halt by a voice raised in question.

"But, Mr. Fortinbras, it says here that profits went up during the last year."

"Total profits did go up slightly, Mrs. Stanton, but they were all from Government Contracts Division."

"I'm afraid I still don't understand." Mrs. Stanton smiled ingratiatingly as her beflowered hat bobbed up and down. "Does that make any difference?"

"Yes, Mrs. Stanton," replied Fortinbras without a hint of exasperation in his voice. A lifetime of teaching had left its mark. "Only one major division was profitable. All the other divisions were run at a loss. Does that clear the point up?"

"Oh, yes." Mrs. Stanton was profuse in her thanks. It was obvious that Fortinbras had reduced her to total bewilderment. To total silence also, with any luck.

The itemization continued, punctuated by similar questions. The two doctors, who had both retired from the cares of medical practice to devote themselves to the management of their estates, were the source of indefatigable interrogation. They seemed to have lived lives singularly untouched by the great stream of national commerce; their oracular manner covered an almost endearing innocence of the Federal tax structure. Fortinbras dealt with them kindly but shortly, and by dint of perseverence came to his peroration.

"These are the areas which should be the subject of meticulous scrutiny. All the basic records have been assembled for my examination, and the preliminary organization has been completed. I will not conceal from you that my worst fears are being substantiated. The financial picture for the present year is a good deal worse than that for the year just past. Incompetence, negligence, stupidity, and obsolescence of both material and personnel are rampant. There is something very radically wrong at National Calculating." He paused for dramatic effect, and everybody looked pleased. If you spend over a thousand dollars for the surgeon, you want the patient to be very ill.

"The final analysis must, of course, await the completion of our investigation. But, with over forty years of experience in this field, I do not think I have ever felt so confident that the outcome will justify my original suspicions. There is no hope of any intelligent or purposive action from the present management which, in my opinion, is composed entirely of incompetents. With your permission and support I am prepared to work on these problems until we can get effective remedies. Our present position is secure. With sufficient persistence we can amass enough data to persuade the Board to take action or to compel the removal of the Board if they refuse to be goaded into activity. I personally am prepared to spend three years at this if necessary. But the final decision must rest with you."

Fortinbras was left in no doubt about the sentiments of the meeting. There was a genteel murmur of approval, joined by the rich young man, who was getting into the spirit of things. Regina Plout rose triumphantly to her feet, assured Fortinbras on behalf of her fellow shareholders of their continued support, and asked for questions from the floor. Thus encouraged, Miriam Dennis, of the envelope-addressing crew, timidly asked Fortinbras if they could look forward to indicting anybody. He very repressively replied that there was no question of instituting criminal proceedings, and the lady resumed her seat, visibly daunted. Mrs. Plout covered the awkward hiatus by announcing that now the business was over, pleasure could begin, and coyly produced a tea trolley laden with coffee and cakes. The gathering rearranged itself into congenial groups, and Fortinbras found himself the focal point of the only three persons present to show any signs of intelligence. Edward Lee was the head of a substantial import business in Chinatown and a power in the Chinese Merchants Association. He had obviously been weaned on financial statements. Mr. and Mrs. Bejamin Adler found time to attend the stockholder meetings although running a successful wholesale lumber business.

"You've got them all excited, Clarence," said Adler, nodding toward the agitated quartet in the corner composed of two doctors and two envelope addressers.

"It's just as well," replied Fortinbras, putting his coffee cup down dubiously on a small marble-top table. "I want them to realize that this may be a long job. The first flush of enthusiasm will die down any day."

"You can count on Mary and me. We trust your intuition, and you probably will uncover something. But what then? Can we really get any action?"

"Well, that depends." Fortinbras rubbed his jaw reflectively. "What I'm afraid is that they'll make only nominal changes. Mason's ready to throw anybody to the wolves. He's quite capable of singling out one division manager and trying to lay the whole mess at his door. But I don't believe that will get to the root of it. Why, there isn't a single person there who isn't ignorant of the simplest principles of cost accounting. No study of break-even points—nothing at all. But we'll have our troubles getting a complete overhaul of the management, and I don't think I'll settle for anything less."

Lee looked thoughtful. "That sounds as if things are worse than we originally anticipated." He looked around to be sure he could not be overheard before continuing. "If they're that bad, Clarence, do you think that there's any chance of fraud, after all? I hadn't considered that possibility."

"There hasn't been any sign of fraud so far, and of course I haven't been thinking along those lines. But I can assure you of this, Edward. The kind of audit that I'm planning will show up everything. If there is fraud, I will find it." Fortinbras's reply was almost a whisper. The ladies were quite excited enough already.

"Well, if you do find it, you're really going to stir up a

hornet's nest." Lee did not seem disturbed by the prospect, but Adler frowned slightly. This was not what he and Mary had bargained for.

"Oh, it will be a hornet's nest all right." Fortinbras's confidence was unshaken. "But I intend to be the hornet."

# 6

# *Fortinbras Rampant*

The convulsions caused by Clarence Fortinbras's activities at National Calculating, together with the publicity —Mrs. Plout had contrived to insert in all the metropolitan papers a snappy little notice of the National Calculating Stockholders' Protest Committee, together with an appeal to other dissatisfied stockholders—were producing talk, if nothing else. At the company, Dr. Morris Richter took one look at the Sidelights Column of *The New York Times* ("Never Underestimate Power of Woman, Corporation Learns"), and hurried off to alarm Allen Hammond by a low-voiced, conspiratorial discussion with vague hints of a corporate coup to oust the reigning powers in favor of younger, more vigorous, if unnamed, staff members. Jay Rutledge, secure in the refuge of the one division that was consistently profitable, tactfully avoided his afflicted fellow division managers, and sought out an old friend, Mrs. Cobb, nominally the assistant division manager to Richter in Research and Development, actually the guiding intelligence in a division notable for the rapid turnover of its chiefs. She listened calmly while he pointed out that Fortinbras was a nuisance underfoot and a public menace, then returned to her Program Evaluation Study. That it would go out under Dr. Richter's signature did not trouble her. Neither did Clarence Fortinbras.

Chip Mason read his morning *Times*, came upon Mrs. Plout's message with a distressed grunt, then talked to Mary

Sullivan about it for forty minutes. When Miss Sullivan was recalled to her duties, he felt the need for further solace.

After some difficulty, he got through to Tom Robichaux.

So it was that John Putnam Thatcher, lunching at the Bankers Club, found himself once again contemplating the dislocations and disruptions occurring at National Calculating. He listened courteously while Robichaux, stopping by after lunch, described the damage being done to the efficient functioning of the corporation's business, the disastrous decline of company morale, the tensions being generated in certain executive offices.

"They'll get used to it," Thatcher said finally. This brutality brought him a look of reproach from Robichaux. "Oh, come now, Tom. They're bound to. Then things will get better."

In point of fact, things got worse, rapidly. The great explosion came not twenty-four hours later. It began on the fifteenth floor.

"Who," demanded Clarence Fortinbras in a voice of barely contained rage, "who has been in here?" His white hair stood in spiky tufts around his face, and his healthy ruddiness was deepened to an unattractive crimson. "Who has been in here?" he repeated, despite the fact that he was completely alone in the hallway into which he had erupted with these peremptory demands. Rigid with indignation, he stood there until Stanley Draper, alerted by the noise, came trotting around the corner, solicitude and deference nicely blended in his approach.

"Did you say something . . ."

"I most certainly did say something," Fortinbras cut him off brutally. "I asked who has been in my office." Impatiently he waved a sheaf of papers under Stanley's nose.

"In here?" Stanley repeated.

"Yes, in here!" Fortinbras snapped. "Somebody has been rooting around in my office." He glowered at Stanley, then apparently awoke to the unkindness of rounding on his lone admirer at National. "Look at it!" Stanley obediently followed him, and inspected the cubicle with anxious curiosity.

Fortinbras had commandeered great piles of National

Calculating's financial reports and records, and they more than filled the small office ungraciously allocated to him. But, as Stanley knew full well, the first duty of the accountant is to seek and maintain order, and Fortinbras had arranged whole cases of papers in meticulous scale of precedence, with brief notes appended to the top copies. "The work, the office, the desk, and the mind are all of a piece," he had told Stanley. "Orderliness is the first requisite."

"You see?" Fortinbras demanded, and Stanley did. Because instead of classic colonnades of ledger heaped on ledger, there was a wild, paper-strewn disorder. Commercial Sales Order Forms (1956-1960), which Fortinbras had made Stanley carefully classify by month, were now jumbled over the table by the window, while Government Contracts Current Vouchers were indiscriminately heaped on some Research and Development Cash Books. Stanley even saw, with a shudder that he concealed by stooping to retrieve them, invoices on the floor.

Fortinbras surveyed the mess. "Yes indeed, someone has been in here, my boy, and someone has taken documents. Not to put too fine a point on it, someone has been looting this office . . ."

"Looting?" Stanley gasped. His allegiance to Fortinbras was unwavering, but a sense of loyalty to National Calculating (and his wife's reminder that his Christmas bonus came from the company) sometimes conflicted with his pursuit of truth in accounting. "Surely not, Mr. Fortinbras. Perhaps somebody wanted to borrow some of the current ledgers. Maybe Mr. Young . . ."

"Stop bleating," Fortinbras said coldly. "Can't you see that someone has removed armfuls of material? By heaven, if they think they can flout a court order . . ." he broke off to stare broodingly at an untidy pile of receipts. Stanley watched apprehensively. Finally Fortinbras made a small noise—between a snort and a grunt—that suggested decision.

"Well, we'll see!"

"See?" Stanley asked. "See what, Mr. Fortinbras?"

"I'm going to talk to Mason," Fortinbras told him grimly.

"Oh, Mr. Fortinbras!" Stanley was appalled.

"I am not going to tolerate this sort of thing," he replied, in an increasingly determined voice. "I have put up with a good deal of willful obstructionism, but this is altogether too much."

He suddenly plunged out into the hall again, followed by Stanley, who was aghast at the turn of events.

"Mr. Fortinbras!" he called after him. "Your suit jacket . . ."

Magnificent in his galluses, his choleric hue alarmingly heightened by a dazzling white shirt, Fortinbras strode down the hall unmindful of the frivolities that exercised smaller minds. The intrusion into his office and the disturbance of his ordered materials was like a personal insult to him. Disdaining the elevator, he mounted the stairs to the sixteenth floor with brisk, decided steps, startling two typists who were precariously balancing milk cartons. They stared at him as he pounded along, the hapless Stanley in his wake.

"Trouble," said Millie laconically.

"Sure thing," said Gloria with no interest.

They were right.

Fortinbras, hitting a pace that winded Stanley, rounded the corner to the president's waiting room, the light of battle in his eye. Stanley not only felt it was his duty to try to avert a scene, he was afraid he might be held responsible for it.

"Perhaps," he cried, "Perhaps if you just asked . . . Mr. Fortinbras! Mr. Fortinbras!"

Mary Sullivan was settling herself at her desk after a thoroughly unsatisfactory luncheon foray to Saks when she heard these trumpetings just as the door to her office was flung open with uncorporate vigor.

"I want to see Mr. Mason!" Fortinbras told her in stentorian tones.

"He has a meeting in twenty minutes," said Mary, startled into a barefaced declaration of the truth.

"Now listen, Mary," he said vehemently, "I want to see Mason, and I don't care if he's got a meeting now!"

Mary liked Fortinbras, who usually treated her with an old-fashioned courtesy that she found charming, if out of place, but she recognized trouble when it stood at her desk; dutifully she tried to pour oil on troubled waters.

"I'll tell him you called, Mr. Fortinbras," she said with a pleasant smile and a look of inquiry at the anguished Stanley, who was grimacing wildly over Fortinbras's shoulder.

"Get me Mason!" bellowed Fortinbras, abandoning old-fashioned manners for simple directness.

"Mr. Fortinbras!"

"Mr. Fortinbras, please . . ."

"What is all this?" The president, sandwich in hand, was drawn from the sanctuary of his office by the unusual uproar; Chip Mason favored plushy quiet. "Oh, Fortinbras," he said unenthusiastically as he incautiously advanced toward Mary Sullivan's desk.

"Yes, Fortinbras," the older man said ferociously. Mason's pink and foolish face goaded him to new heights of fury. "And let me tell you that if you think that you can steal your way out of trouble, you're mistaken . . ."

"Steal?" Mason said confusedly. "Steal? What are you talking about? What's he talking about, Miss Sullivan?"

Mary saw that her employer's manner was not calculated to soothe Fortinbras, whatever might be bothering him, and she hastily tried to fling herself into the widening breach.

"I was just trying to find out," she said brightly, but Fortinbras waved her to a halt.

"I'll tell you what this is all about," he shouted. "Someone around here is a thief. He's stolen the records . . ."

These words penetrated Mason's formidable defenses. "Oh, look here, Fortinbras," he said stiffly, "I'm sorry to have to tell you that you're going just a little too far . . ."

"Try not to be a bigger fool than God made you," Fortinbras said nastily. "Somebody has been looting my office— Stanley here can tell you that—and I want to know what you propose to do."

"Draper," Mason grasped the familiar in a sea of confusion. The younger man jumped slightly.

"S-sir?"

"Just what is all this about? Have you seen anybody in Mr. Fortinbras's office?" He spoke in the kindly avuncular tone appropriate for junior staff.

"I didn't see anything," Stanley said unhappily, with a

worried glance at Fortinbras who was rising onto his toes as he prepared for combat. "That is, I was working in my office . . ."

"There you are," Mason said turning to Fortinbras with a satisfied smile. "Young Draper here didn't see anybody— damn it, man, there wasn't anybody. Everybody was at lunch . . ."

"Listen to me," Fortinbras said savagely. "Are you capable of understanding even very simple statements? Somebody has entered my office and removed several important papers. I demand . . ."

"Now look here, Fortinbras," said Mason, not without dignity. "You heard Draper. And, I need hardly remind you, we are not thieves at National Calculating . . ."

"Oh, no?" said Fortinbras unpleasantly. "Do you suppose that those papers disappeared by themselves?"

"You probably misplaced them," Mason was stung into retorting unwisely. "You have half the corporate files in there . . ."

"Misplaced them!" Fortinbras repeated, genuinely shocked by the suggestion. "Are you mad? I don't misplace papers!" In his rage he gave a curious little hopping motion vaguely suggestive of a native war dance.

"What is all this?" demanded Harry Blaney, shrugging on his overcoat. He emerged from his office at the end of the hallway and approached the group, eying Fortinbras's gesticulations with incomprehension. "Having a little excitement here?" he asked with automatic geniality before he got down to his business. "Mary, I'm going to lunch now. Tell Janice that I'll be back in about an hour and a half . . ."

"Ah-hah!" Fortinbras said, pointing a finger at him. "There you are. Mr. Blaney!"—and there was some sarcasm in the title—"Mr. Blaney was in the building. And now that I come to think of it, I saw you downstairs, didn't I, Mr. Blaney?"

Blaney looked blankly at him. "Went down to see the accountants about some expense account trouble," he said vaguely. "Ask Janice to get that memorandum done this afternoon, will you, Mary?" Finally he was struck by the quality of the silence that surrounded him. "Say," he said looking up again, "what is this?"

"Mr. Fortinbras," said Mason, choking slightly on the name, "Mr. Fortinbras thinks that someone has stolen papers from his room."

"Mr. Fortinbras knows that someone has stolen papers," Fortinbras corrected him.

"Oh, sure," Blaney said, with a knowing look at Mason. "Well, that's the way things go, Fortinbras." He glanced at his watch. "Sorry I can't stay to join the clambake, but I've got an important meeting."

"Harry!" called Mason, who felt the need for support.

"Come back here!" Fortinbras cried.

But Blaney was halfway down the hall. They looked after him with expressions that nearly brought a smile to Mary Sullivan's face.

"I can well understand the chaos in your corporate finances and your business outlook," Fortinbras said in a lowered but still unfriendly voice, "if that is a sample of the best upper-level executive you can get."

Mason was inclined to agree, but he was not going to let Fortinbras call the tune. "I see no reason for Mr. Blaney to waste his time," he retorted icily, "to waste time, I repeat, dealing with these irresponsible and childish accusations . . ."

"Irresponsible?" squeaked Fortinbras, pounding a fist on Mary's desk. "Irresponsible? I am going to get to the bottom of this mess—I repeat, mess. And you are not going to stop me. If I have to padlock my office, I will. If you people— you and Blaney—think that you can abscond . . ."

"Now stop right there," Mason interrupted, thoughtlessly jamming the sandwich he had been clutching onto a folder on Mary's desk. "I have tried to be as courteous and helpful as possible in the circumstances, but I am not going to put up with cheap sneers and . . ."

"Oh, you're not!"

"No, I'm not! And if you want to bandy accusations . . ."

". . . completely incompetent . . ."

". . . crank and troublemaker . . ."

Battle was now joined, and while Mary and Stanley looked on helplessly, Mason and Fortinbras went at it hammer and tongs "Mr. Mason," Mary pleaded "Please, Mr. Mason." But it was to no avail. The accumulated aggravations of the last week had seethed to the surface; both men were beside themselves. "Oh, Mr. Fortinbras," cried Stanley, ineffectually wringing his hands; he could not delude himself that his part in the fracas was likely to lead to advancement. "Mr. Fortinbras!"

"Let them fight," snapped Mary finally, with none of her normal good temper. "Let them scream like fishwives!" The description was apt; Mason, a man habitually responsive to any show of force, was for once flicked on the raw, and like a cornered rabbit was raging with a strength beyond his wont. Fortinbras, Mary saw at a glance, was an old warrior, reveling in combat, and, she would guess, usually successful at it.

Their voices had risen to an inhuman mechanical level when Allen Hammond and Morris Richter strolled into the office, and stopped dead in their tracks. Mary pushed a lock of hair from her forehead and, for once abandoning the businesslike manner she prided herself on, turned to greet them with genuine relief. Allen Hammond, in fact, took an instinctive step toward her, a smiling question in his eyes.

"Allen, do something," she hissed. She might have shouted for all that the combatants would have noticed.

"Good God!" he said tearing his eyes from her as he resumed his advance into the room, Richter at his heels. He looked startled and slightly amused at the amount of noise that Fortinbras and Mason were creating. "What is this?"

Pausing to catch his breath, Mason noticed the newcomers. "This madman claims that somebody has been stealing his papers. Stealing, do you hear me!" he stuttered.

"Madman, is it?" roared Fortinbras.

"Please, Mr. Mason, do control yourself," Mary said.

"Uncle Chas," Hammond said, taken aback by Mason's uncharacteristic forcefulness.

"I tell you the man's a raving idiot," said Chip Mason. "I'm not going to put up with it."

Both Allen and Mary were standing fascinated by the un-expected determination in Mason's voice when Richter con-tributed his mite to the exchange. "Did Fortinbras find anything wrong with the books?" he asked in a stage whisper of nobody at all. His serious face was composed into an ex-pression of considered inquiry. Mason was about to blast him, when Hammond roused himself.

"Now let's just calm down," he said with an air of com-mand that his uncle envied. "Exactly what is the matter, sir?" he asked, turning to Fortinbras courteously.

The calm good sense of his voice was not without effect. Mason took a deep breath, and Fortinbras, remembering himself, grasped the opportunity to abandon the slanging match with Mason.

"I'll tell you what's the matter," he said, forcefully but with control. "Somebody has entered my office and purloined some papers."

Richter then undid Allen's good work by allowing himself a professorial chuckle.

" 'Purloined,' " he said lightly when they turned to look at him. "It's a rather odd word, isn't it?"

"Oh, you find it amusing?" said Fortinbras, reinvigorated by this fresh folly. "Well, let me tell you that there is nothing funny about the fact that somebody has entered my office, disrupted my carefully arranged work, and stolen—yes, Mr. Mason, I said stolen—papers. Your uncle tells me that no one was on the premises, and I discover Mr. Blaney lurking around! This is an attempt to interrupt, if not to disrupt en-tirely, my work, and I have no intention . . ."

"Surely," Hammond interrupted persuasively, while Mary and Stanley suppressed groans, "surely," he continued, "there isn't any real evidence of theft. And then, there is no real reason to steal papers . . ."

"Young man," began Fortinbras, his voice again mounting with emotion, when another spectator drifted up. Mrs. Cobb, coming into the front office on some errand, stopped short at the door.

"What's the matter?" she asked with a slightly alarmed glance at the popeyed expression worn by Mason. She did not raise her voice, but again the intrusion of a newcomer shifted the focus of attention. "Has there been an accident?" she asked, advancing into the room.

"There has not been an accident," said Fortinbras, who had a gift for seizing the initiative. "There has been a crime!"

She raised her eyebrows as if deprecating the violence with which he spoke, but he turned back to Mason. "And I insist, do you hear me? I insist that you take immediate steps to investigate this—this outrage."

This ultimatum—and no one could deny it was one—was followed by a pregnant silence. Mason, his hands shaking, opened his mouth, then shut it, still incapable of controlling his furious anger at Fortinbras's accusations. Hammond, frankly puzzled, was casting looks of inquiry at Mary Sullivan who was taut with disapproval. Richter, rendered wary by Fortinbras's attack on him, maintained a prudent silence, while Stanley Draper was simply unhappy. Only Mrs. Cobb remained self-possessed. She was about to press for further details, when an unhappy fate intervened.

Its pawn was Barney Young, Assistant Division Manager of Government Contracts, a rotund, placid man, normally slow of movement and restrained in his speech.

"You're all here," he cried joyfully as he burst into the room, an idiotic smile on his round face. Grinning broadly, he advanced, unaware that he was a breath of fresh air blowing over smoldering embers. "Here!" he cried happily, pushing a large cigar from the box he brandished into Fortinbras's outstretched hand. "Congratulate me! It's a boy! And after six girls!" he chuckled contentedly, his own delight blinding him to the singular lack of response from his co-workers. "I looked in this morning, but you weren't here, Chip, and I certainly want you to have one of these extraspecial seegars. Here, Mary, take one. You can always give one to your young man. Eight pounds, you know, and he was a week late. . . ." His voice trailed off as he registered the strained expressions surrounding him.

"Adele is fine, the doctor said," he added in a slightly plaintive voice. Mary summoned a wan smile, but Fortinbras unceremoniously thrust the cigar back at him.

"Cigars!" he said with heavy irony. "Babies! Idiots in Commercial Sales. And a front office that is totally devoid of the most rudimentary common sense." His voice was offensively even, as he recited this catalogue of offenses.

"Oh, now look here," said Young, hurt.

Fortinbras ignored him. "Well, there's obviously nothing to be gained trying to get a modicum of cooperation from you," he told Mason, who glared at him. "Or you"—he added, waving an inclusive hand over the group he was including in his indictment. "I suppose I should not be surprised. This is not the first act of dishonesty, I might even say of deliberate criminal fraud that this management has perpetrated, and you can tell Blaney! But if you think that you can continue these felonious activities of yours . . ."

"Nonsense!" Mrs. Cobb said in sharp reproof. He turned to look at her. "There is no need to make a scene," she said with crisp disapproval.

He emitted an angry bark of laughter. "Quite right," he said. "No need at all. Just don't think that this sort of thing is going to stop me, that's all!"

Majestically dismissing them, he turned on his heel and strode from the room, leaving his adversaries gaping openmouthed after him. Stanley Draper hesitated a moment, then, after a harassed look at Mason, scurried after him.

"Well!" said Richter, breaking the silence that Fortinbras left.

"The man is a lunatic," Mason said. "A complete lunatic. He's misplaced a paper in that warren of his, and he's gone completely berserk . . ."

"I expect you're right," Allen said agreeably, but with a speculative look in his eye as he settled himself on the corner of Mary's desk. "I mean, there's no possible reason to believe that anybody did steal anything, is there? Sorry, we came in rather late . . ."

"There is not," Mason shouted. He looked down at the sandwich now crushed beyond recall on the desk. "I'm going to get to work," he said, making no move to leave.

"You know," Richter commented with a judicious impartiality that jarred several of his listeners, "I wouldn't be surprised if it wasn't his age. Old people do tend to get forgetful. I know that Fortinbras is—or was—a perfectly competent sort of chap. I wouldn't be surprised if he isn't getting a little past his work. That would account for the emotionality of this outburst."

Under normal conditions, this dispassion would have raised Mason's hackles, but he was in such sympathy with the sentiments that he nodded eagerly.

"I believe you're right," he said. "He's just forgotten what he did with something, and then he blew up. It's really a little hard on us . . ." His commanding tones of anger were giving way to his usual petulance. "I don't suppose we can expect an apology from him, though. I certainly think we deserve one, let me tell you!"

Thankfully Mary Sullivan sank into her chair; her knees were somewhat weak. She carefully avoided looking at Allen Hammond, who was regarding her in a fashion disturbingly destructive of her view of the way the Perfect Secretary should treat the President's Nephew, and instead listened carefully to Richter and Mason who were convincing themselves that Fortinbras had lost a paper.

She did not think that he was the careless type.

Neither, she saw from her expression, did Mrs. Cobb.

Barney Young looked downcast.

"Oh, Mr. Young," she said. "I'm so glad."

This recalled the senior staff to their obligations.

"Congratulations, Barney, old man . . ."

". . . nice going, Barney . . ."

# 7

# *Fortinbras Fuit*

It is not publicly admitted, but behind every chaste earnings statement reported in the financial press lies a human drama. It may be a power struggle between executive vice president and senior vice president, it may be a four-million-dollar loss in an Italian subsidiary caused by the boneheadedness of the treasurer, it may be a broken contract, an alcoholic buying agent, or simply an inconvenient heart attack. Good or bad, it is there, part of the great human comedy.

The men behind the numbers become worthy of newspaper comment only if that human comedy includes horses, spectacular blondes, or unexpected trips to Brazil.

Nevertheless, people know. Whether you dignify it as "inside information," or call it "what they are saying on the Street," rumor penetrates into board rooms as fast as it crosses the backyard fence.

John Thatcher was therefore by no means surprised to find the troubles of National Calculating becoming public—or semipublic—property. Fortinbras's eruption into Mason's office was a case in point. Within four hours he received a detailed description of the scene. He was to keep it under his hat, said Tom Robichaux confidentially, but there it was. Wouldn't do to let the news get around but, frankly, things were looking worse and worse. Robichaux and Devane didn't like it at all.

"I can understand that," said Thatcher astringently. He heard Robichaux out for another two minutes of lamentation, then replaced the phone and turned to his subordinate, Charlie Trinkam, the most rakish element in the Sloan's generally sedate staff.

"That accountant over at National?" Charlie asked easily. "Heard he's really after them. They had some sort of big blowup in the front office today."

"How did you find out so fast?"

Charlie grinned and reported that in the interests of the Sloan's investment in National Calculating—here he shook his head sadly—he was cultivating a young physicist employed by National. "Says, by the way, that the real brains in the lab is this Cobb woman. Richter is just another Boy Genius."

"And your physicist isn't a boy genius?" Thatcher asked idly, turning his attention to Trinkam's long report on the profit possibilities inherent in a nuclear power station situated in Armonk.

Charlie was indignant. "My physicist is named Celia."

Thatcher should have known.

The next morning Walter Bowman buttonholed him at the end of an Investment Committee meeting and, drawing him aside, gave him a substantially accurate account of the scene.

"Do you know Celia too?" Thatcher inquired.

Bowman, a devoted husband and proud father of three children whom he rarely saw, looked puzzled. "Who's Celia? No, I ran into a fellow I know over there . . ." His voice trailed away vaguely. Unlike Trinkam, he liked to protect his sources.

Thatcher watched the last of the Investment Committee trail out of the conference room. Burton Claster, whose secretary had twice interrupted the meeting with urgent telephone calls, was continuing his impersonation of important man of affairs with a magisterial frown at something that Trinkam was saying.

"Well, I wish we weren't in National," Bowman continued. "This guy Rutledge is the only one who can handle Fortinbras, and he wasn't at the fight. Busy taking their tame general to lunch. A lot depends on that government contract, you know."

Thatcher tore his attention away from Claster. "I'm glad somebody at National is attending to business," he said, joining Bowman on the way to the elevator. "From what I hear, very little hard work is being done. Except by Clarence Fortinbras."

"It's been like that for a long time at National," said Walter Bowman. "They've got nowhere to go but up."

But intelligence flowing from the scene of battle during the next three weeks did not confirm this guarded optimism. Stories of sweeping raids on files, stories of President Charles Mason's frenzied descents on lawyers, stories of emergency meetings, percolated to the Sloan, to the Security Analysts Luncheon Association, to the brokerage houses.

"Heard the latest about National?" inquired Thatcher's neighbor at a meeting of the Advisory Committee of the Lower Broad Street Committee.

This was less surprising than it might seem. Giles Conrad was a partner at Amos Durleth, Exchange Specialists.

"I had hoped so," said Thatcher. This did not spare him a long anecdote centering on National Calculating's Division Manager of Commercial Sales who had, said Conrad, blown up.

"Blown up?" asked Thatcher, wishing the waiter would provide more coffee.

Harry Blaney had claimed that Clarence Fortinbras was not conducting a normal audit, but something more like an invasion by the Russian Army.

"He tells me that the man has bags and bags of canceled checks," said Conrad, shuddering slightly. Thatcher eyed the head table. There was trouble with the loudspeaker.

"And he said that now Fortinbras is talking about going over to New Jersey to take an actual physical inventory." Conrad paused to let Thatcher comment.

"Nasty implications," said Thatcher.

"Very nasty," Conrad agreed. "Blaney says he told Mason that that was going too far. Of course he's in a bad spot, not making money . . ."

"Mason?"

"No, Blaney."

Thatcher agreed that this cut Blaney's bargaining position. He was spared the need to say anything further.

"LADIES AND GENTLEMEN!" the loudspeaker thundered.

"General Radio makes those damned things," Conrad confided. Thatcher made a mental note to talk to Walter Bowman about General Radio.

In the midst of this welter of speculation, John Thatcher fully expected an SOS from Tom Robichaux.

He got it the next morning, while he was dictating to Miss Corsa. In tones of deep depression, Robichaux reported that (1) Fortinbras was exceeding the mandate of his court order, (2) he was raising hell on the premises, and (3) he was endangering the United States Government contract on which Jay Rutledge, National Calculating—and Robichaux and Devane—were counting.

"Yes?" said Thatcher watching Miss Corsa check her transcription.

"And Chip needs help," said Robichaux.

"Tell him to try the lawyers."

"Lawyers!" Robichaux's tones of loathing reminded Thatcher that the divorce had slipped his mind. But Robichaux did not swerve course. "Friendly offices, that's what he wants. You and me—we could go over and talk to Fortinbras."

"Look, Tom, it isn't any of our business . . . no, I don't mean our financial commitment . . . What? Well, of course, if you really think it would help. Fortinbras is willing? . . . All right. Tomorrow afternoon then."

He replaced the phone rather guiltily. Miss Corsa was expressionless.

"I am not, as you no doubt think, Miss Corsa, simply yielding to curiosity. It is possible, remotely possible, that Robichaux and I may do something to help."

"I'll make a note of the appointment," said Miss Corsa.

He could tell from her tone that she had seen through him. Curiosity, Miss Corsa believed, killed the cat.

The next day, when he met Robichaux uptown, Thatcher was inclined to think that Miss Corsa might be right. For

Tom Robichaux was clearly in a very bad mood. He was awesomely silent during their taxi ride to the Southern Bourbon Building. When Miss Sullivan ushered them into Mason's office and promised to produce the absent president, he did not eye her trim figure but instead threw his overcoat onto the aggressively masculine leather sofa with a discontented grunt.

"National," he grumbled as he stalked to the window, "is taking up too damn much of my time. When these nutboys start crawling out of the woodwork . . ."

Thatcher broke into the bad-tempered rumble. "What are you talking about, Tom?"

"I said," Tom replied, abandoning the scenery as he returned to sink heavily into a chair opposite Thatcher, "things are going from bad to worse. Sometimes I think it's about time to get out of business. God knows, it isn't worth-while anymore. There are these crazy stockholders—why, John, I remember when they wouldn't have dared to open their mouths. And the SEC! And if you do make a dollar, you have to give the government a dollar seventy-five." He broke off and looked indignantly at Thatcher. "What's funny?"

This jeremiad, lacking form and shape, had enlightened John Thatcher.

"I take it you're having trouble with Dorothy's lawyer," he said, responding to the spirit, if not the content of the outburst.

Tom was about to protest, then, with an automatically furtive look around the office, unbent. "Trouble?" he repeated sourly. "My God, you wouldn't believe it. That woman wants the sun, the moon, and the stars. At cost."

"Is she going to get them?"

Robichaux pounded his knee with a clenched fist. "She is not," he said determinedly. "But—and I wouldn't tell anyone else about this, John—she's got these countercharges. Hell," he said in a burst of candor, "She's trying to blackmail me."

Thatcher was not unduly surprised, having heard the same story of Eileen, whatshername and Ruby. Ruby, the mistake of a younger and less experienced Robichaux, was the only one of his wives to trounce him during separation negotiations. She now lived expensively in the south of France. Thatcher had a well-placed confidence in Tom's ability to extricate himself, relatively unscathed, from whatever difficulties Dorothy could raise.

". . . so I said, publish and be damned." Robichaux said with a hopeful look. A comment was clearly in order.

"Not very original, Tom, but I suppose it was effective."

Robichaux leaned back and considered this. "Well," he said, "we're going to see. I'm a pretty optimistic sort, myself, you know." Thatcher did indeed. ". . . but first Dewey and then Nixon . . . that shook me . . ."

"What do you mean, Dewey and Nixon shook you?" Thatcher demanded.

"They taught me not to take anything for granted . . . Still, I'm optimistic." He pulled out a watch chain, consulted a Philippe Patek designed expressly for upper-income vest pockets, and abandoned self-analysis. "Where the hell is Chip?"

From his tone, Thatcher saw that Tom was here in his capacity as senior partner of Robichaux and Devane, underwriter to National Calculating Corporation, rather than as an old friend of Chip Mason. If anything, his friendship with that unfortunate man seemed to harshen his judgments. They sat for another few moments in silence, then Robichaux spoke again. "You wouldn't think that one of the great quarterbacks of all time would be so spineless, would you?"

"Tennis is my game," Thatcher replied. "What do you mean, spineless?"

"I mean that if Chip had shown any spirit, he wouldn't be in this mess, and we wouldn't be sitting here wasting our time." Again he consulted the timepiece.

"It takes more than spirit to raise your earnings," Thatcher commented fair-mindedly. "Mind you, I'd be the first to admit that Mason is no Geneen . . ."

"Geneen! He's not half the man his father was," said Robichaux brutally. "And the Old Man was selling cash registers. If Chip could handle these fancy computers of his as well as the Old Man handled cash registers everything would be just fine. Mind you, National's basically sound." He jumped impatiently to his feet and stamped to the window. "That crazy Fortinbras," he said over his shoulder. "Why couldn't Chip get rid of the loony? Dammit, the Old Man . . ."

"Now wait a minute, Tom," Thatcher said. "In the first place, stop pretending that Fortinbras is a typical stockholder nuisance. You know as well as I do that he's a high-powered dealer, and it would take a better man than Chip Mason to brush him off."

Robichaux opened his mouth to protest, but Thatcher continued inexorably. "And he had a court order. Leaving aside the implications of that—for National's underwriters, say, who might be presumed to have investigated a company they were interested in—you know as well as I do that Chip Mason had no alternative but to let Fortinbras see the books. And Fortinbras," he said in a reflective tone that grated on Robichaux's ears—"Fortinbras seems to be having a field day with them, doesn't he?"

Robichaux accepted these comments in a darkling silence. That his impatient pacing was accompanied by thought was revealed a few moments later.

"Court order," he said, seizing the crux of the matter. "You know these Democrats are going to ruin the capitalistic system!"

Thus when Chip Mason, full of apologies, breathlessly hurried into his office, his affronted eyes were met with the spectacle of his major creditor roaring with laughter, and his most important underwriter looking thoroughly bewildered.

"Well, I'm glad you've got something to smile about, Thatcher," he said plaintively after the appropriate greetings had been exchanged. "Isn't Fortinbras here yet? I'm just as glad. I need to get my breath for a minute. I tell you, between trying to calm Blaney down, and working with those damned lawyers, I don't know what I'm doing. It's . . . oh, thanks, Mary."

That Mason did not know what he was doing, Thatcher could well believe as he watched him thank Mary Sullivan for the glass of milk she put on the desk. There was real

warmth in the bobbing of his head at her, not the perfunc-
tory, mechanical acknowledgment usually affected by the
man of affairs. Chip Mason was a man who was born to have
somebody else do something. As the amiable, if vacuous son
of a forceful father for most of his life—except for his fleeting
gridiron fame—he had never developed the capacity to meet
an emergency.

And emergency it clearly was. Mason tossed off his milk,
and continued his revealing confidences. "He's driving us all
crazy, here. I don't know how we're going to get our production going while he's running around upsetting everything. You know our big Army contract is coming up for
renewal this month, Tom, and there's no doubt about our
getting it—after all, we're the only TCR producer in the
country—but it's a busy time for all of us. Jay has his hands
full almost every day with General Cartwright. Thank God
he was taking him out to lunch the time that Fortinbras went
crazy and accused us of being thieves! But naturally we
want to make a good impression on the General. If this Fortinbras goes on . . ."

"Now take it easy," said Robichaux with sudden magisterial calm, his assurance restored by the sight of someone
more upset than he. Mason looked up at him with eager expectation. "We'll just talk turkey to him . . ."

"I don't like to interrupt," Thatcher said dryly, "but where
is Mr. Fortinbras? I thought this was a conference, not a
conspiracy."

Robichaux was prepared to expostulate when Thatcher
continued. "Be sensible, Tom! We're here to try to help
straighten up this mess." He saw Mason wince slightly. "It's
not going to get us off on the right foot if Fortinbras arrives
to find us with our heads together."

His comment rattled Mason, who looked alarmed, but
Robichaux nodded approval. "You're right."

"Yes, where is he?" Mason complained nervously. He
stabbed at his buzzers. "Mary? Do you know where that . . ."
He caught Thatcher's stern eye on him and hastily shifted
gears. ". . . where Mr. Fortinbras is? What? Well, keep try-

ing and tell him that Mr. Robichaux and Mr. Thatcher are waiting."

He presented Thatcher and Robichaux with the pleased smile of a child whose performance has gone well. Thatcher felt a sudden sympathy for the realistic Fortinbras, whose travails had undoubtedly included prolonged exposure to Mason's vapidity.

They sat in awkward silence.

"Well," Robichaux said heavily.

More silence.

"I got the invitation to your football dinner, Chip," Thatcher said conversationally.

"What?" Mason bleated. He was listening for footsteps. "Oh, the dinner." Momentarily, he forgot his troubles. A brief gleam of enthusiasm lit his pale eyes. "Yes, it's going to be a great evening. You know Bull Peabody is coming down?"

Thatcher did not, but the news bestirred Robichaux. "How is Bull?" he asked. Dehavilland Peabody, a leader of the conservative coalition in the United States Senate, would always be known to at least some Harvard men as Bull. Recalling one of his afterdinner speeches at the University Club, Thatcher reflected that the name was not entirely inapposite.

". . . unless there's a committee meeting," Mason said, his attention again wandering from the conversation. "You see what I mean?" he suddenly hissed across the desk at them. "Fellow doesn't even show up for a conference!"

Robichaux nodded, and Mason, fighting strong emotion, leaned back and drummed on the armrest.

They waited another tedious ten minutes.

Mary Sullivan, sticking her head in the door, was irresistibly reminded of a still life. By John Singer Sargent, for instance.

"We can't seem to find Mr. Fortinbras," she reported.

"Isn't he in his office?" Mason demanded.

To Thatcher's admiration, Miss Sullivan's control in the face of this question remained perfect. "I've just been down there," she explained to the intent Mason. "Mr. Fortinbras

isn't at his desk. But we'll find him, Mr. Mason." The soothing note in her voice was not lost on Thatcher, who smiled
to himself as he watched her depart. His own Miss Corsa
tended to reproach rather than comfort, but there appeared
to be a natural law of compensation. Where there was a
void—and Thatcher felt no hesitation in describing Mason as
just that—some mysterious force provided a Miss Sullivan.
Probably the only thing that saved the capitalist system.

"I knew we should have lunched with him," one of its
stoutest defenders grumbled. "It doesn't make sense to meet
people after lunch. People are always sleepy, or late. Fellow's
probably just finishing a steak somewhere."

"He's not a great eater, as I recall," Thatcher said pro-
vocatively. It was now two-thirty, and he resigned himself
to deriving what amusement he could from the meeting.
"He's probably checking some figures at the last minute . . ."

"You know what I mean . . ."

Robichaux's comment, and Mason's anxiety at Thatcher's
pleasantry, were rudely and dramatically interrupted. The
door to Mason's office was abruptly flung open, and as they
turned to stare, a young man, gasping for breath, propped
himself up with an outstretched arm and looked wildly at
them. Over his shoulder peered Mary Sullivan, shocked and
for once at a loss.

Surprisingly, it was Mason who found tongue first. "Dr.
Richter," he said with no more than grievance in his voice,
"I'm having a meeting." His banker's mind functioning quite
automatically, Thatcher instantly wrote off the Sloan's investment in National Calculating Corporation.

"He's dead," Richter gasped. His eyes were watering, and
there was a queer, pinched look about his nostrils.

"Dead!" squeaked Mason, startled out of his trance. "Who's
dead?"

Before Richter supplied the name, Thatcher knew the
answer.

But Chip Mason and Tom Robichaux appeared to be surprised.

"Fortinbras," gasped Richter, who was getting his second

wind. Speechlessly, they stared at him, and he realized that some explanation was necessary.

"I was coming back from lunch," he said. He stopped short, and passed a hand in front of his eyes. When he continued there was a note of supplication in his voice. "I thought I'd talk to Fortinbras. You know"—he was addressing Mason, who stared open-mouthed—"you know, I thought it might be helpful to make him see our point of view. It wouldn't do any harm if some of us got to know him a little better . . ."

"I don't think that's a good idea," Mason began censoriously.

"My God!" Robichaux burst out.

"Get on with your story," Thatcher directed. The hysterical note in Richter's voice had not escaped him.

"Well," Richter said quickly, "He's wasn't there. And I went in to leave a note on his desk. Then I found him." He swallowed convulsively.

"Found him?" Mason repeated dreamily.

"He was lying behind his desk. You couldn't see him from the hall, that's why I thought the office was empty. He had a cord wrapped around his neck, and his face . . ." he broke off and shocked his audience by a noise between a whimper and a giggle. "It was the cord from the adding machine on his desk!"

Richter's evident intention to give way to tortured laughter was foiled by John Thatcher, who quite suddenly decided that he had had enough drama from the staff of National Calculating Corporation.

"Did you call the police?" he snapped, reaching across the immobilized Mason for the phone. "How do you dial outside?" He found Mary Sullivan at his side, reaching for the phone.

"I'll do it," she said crisply.

Mason was frozen in his chair; Robichaux, ferocious with disapproval, had not moved; and Richter had sagged against the wall, pushed there by the redoubtable Miss Sullivan.

"Police?" asked Richter confusedly.

"Police!" Mason whispered.

"Now, John," Robichaux awoke to say. "Maybe you're being a little hasty . . ."

Miss Sullivan was ignoring these comments, Thatcher noted approvingly. "Maybe I am," he said irascibly. "But when you find a man who has been murdered, it is customary to inform the police."

Mary Sullivan looked up at this, but continued her low-voiced exchange on the phone. The rest of his audience was momentarily stilled by his observation. Then the president of National Calculating Corporation found voice.

"I wish," he said forcefully, "I wish that Fortinbras would drop dead!"

# 8

# *Weepings and Lamentations*

Death, which was the end for Clarence Fortinbras, was only the beginning for John Thatcher. After the initial shock, he braced himself for an afternoon marked by assorted idiocies from the senior management of National Calculating Corporation. His expectations were more than fulfilled.

Chip Mason, upon absorbing the nature of the event which had occurred—a process requiring the united explanatory efforts of Thatcher, Tom Robichaux, and Miss Sullivan—had been unable to restrain his satisfaction.

"At least this means that lunatic won't be messing around the office any more."

"Chip, don't be silly," warned Jay Rutledge sharply. The Southerner had been hastily summoned by Mary Sullivan. "This is going to give the newspapers a carnival. We're in for the worst time we've ever had at National. Reporters will be swarming around these offices."

Shocked into silence by this display of irritation from Jay Rutledge, Mason retired to a corner to nurse his grievances and his ulcer. The afternoon, which for Thatcher early assumed the dreamy proportions of a nightmare, remained fixed in his memory as an unending procession of glasses of milk borne ceremoniously to the presidential desk.

Harry Blaney, who could not be found on the premises, arrived forty-five minutes later, demanding an explanation for the presence of the police. Upon being told of the murder, he embarked on a nervous protestation of innocence which won him a puzzled look from Allen Hammond and the sinister assurance: "Don't worry, Harry, we'll all stick behind you," from Kellog, the general counsel.

Naturally unnerved by this remark, Blaney launched into a comprehensive accusation which embraced the entire gathering and suggested a two-pronged conspiracy directed against himself and Fortinbras. The inclusion of Fortinbras as a fellow victim was clearly an afterthought. This provoked a heated reply from Mason which centered on Blaney's managerial incompetence, and included a fairly accurate reproduction of Blaney's ominous remarks about the victim two days before his murder. The entire exchange was recorded for posterity by a police guard seated in the corner, and brought to an end only by a surprising display of white-lipped acerbity on the part of Mrs. Cobb who roundly ordered all the participants into silence.

Morris Richter was sick in the executive men's room.

Four hours passed before a heavily patient lieutenant from the Homicide Squad summed up the results of his afternoon's work.

"All right then. It looks as if nobody here has an alibi except Mr. Thatcher and Mr. Robichaux." He surveyed the group with dissatisfaction. "Kind of funny, that. It would save a lot of trouble if you people ate lunch together." There was no response. Perhaps it occurred to the lieutenant that, from what he had seen, the suspects would not have made particularly congenial dining companions. He sighed heavily. "I guess you two can go. We may be here quite a while longer."

Thatcher needed no urging. Ignoring the mute appeal of Charles Mason and the suddenly stricken glance of Mrs. Cobb, he took a prompt and enthusiastic departure. But an evening spent with Robichaux who was, by turn, affronted or oppressed, did nothing to lift his spirits. Unable to abandon a topic irritating to both, they went over the same ground again and again. The situation at National and the peculiar talents of Clarence Fortinbras led to only one conclusion.

"Things up there must be worse than I thought," said Tom sadly as his taxi deposited Thatcher in front of the Devonshire. "The bottom of the market will drop out."

"You and your old friends!"

Thatcher fondly hoped that his return to the Sloan the next morning, with a change in venue and personnel, would give his thoughts a cheerier direction. But he failed to reckon with the powerful attraction which the murder of Clarence Fortinbras exerted on the imaginations of his colleagues and the rest of the population of New York. Within an hour of his arrival at least a dozen of his associates made their way into his office on the most barefaced pretexts, seeking an eyewitness account of what the *Herald Tribune,* in its misguided search for an airy prose style, called the "corporate garroting" of Clarence Fortinbras. Thatcher was in no mood to satisfy these demands. Dealing tactfully but firmly with Brad Withers, president of the Sloan, and just as firmly, if not quite so tactfully, with a glittering-eyed Everett Gabler (who thought the whole thing was "an unprecedented outrage"), he turned to his secretary and firmly announced that he was unavailable to all visitors.

"And that means all! I don't care if it's the chairman of the board, Miss Corsa."

"Yes, Mr. Thatcher," she replied obediently.

Thatcher decided that he had undervalued Miss Corsa during the past two years. Phlegmatic she might be. But she was also devoid of all curiosity as to the manner of Clarence Fortinbras's demise.

"What about the newspapers, Mr. Thatcher?" she asked in an uninterested voice.

"What newspapers?" he asked suspiciously, visualizing a horde of reporters in the foyer six stories below.

"The *Times* and the *Wall Street Journal*," she replied reproachfully, "You always look at them."

"Oh, yes. Give them to me."

He carried the two periodicals back with him and spread them out on his desk. The *Times* had a two-column headline below the fold. Very decent, all things considered. Nevertheless, he thought with growing dissatisfaction, he remembered a day when that august journal did not recognize the existence of crime. Standards were slipping everywhere.

### NOTED ACCOUNTANT SLAIN
### ON MADISON AVENUE

#### CLARENCE FORTINBRAS
#### STRANGLED AT
#### NATIONAL CALCULATING

November 8, New York.—The body of Clarence Fortinbras, a prominent certified public accountant, was discovered in the accounting department of National Calculating Corporation at 375 Madison Avenue this afternoon. Mr. Fortinbras had been strangled with an electrical cord during the lunch hour. The victim was conducting an examination of the financial accounts of National Calculating as representative of a stockholders' group which has been dissatisfied with the management of the corporation and has secured a court order to conduct an audit.

There followed an exhaustive analysis of the litigation between Clarence Fortinbras and Charles Mason, including extended quotations from the text of the court order, and a lengthy biography of Fortinbras. Thatcher was interested to discover that Fortinbras had been called in during the Tucker liquidation and for the reorganization at Inland Steel. The article concluded with statements by everybody at National Calculating.

"National Calculating is shocked and appalled," said Charles Mason, president of National Calculating. "We are convinced that some personal enemy of Mr. Fortinbras made his way onto the premises and committed this crime. The police shall receive every assistance from my staff." Jay Rutledge had contented himself with remarking that it was a terrible tragedy, and National Calculating was at a loss to

explain the occurrence. Morris Richter had said that everybody was displaying commendable calm, Harry Blaney said
that Fortinbras was a sad loss to the accounting profession,
and Dr. Margaret Cobb had refused to comment. Thatcher
was sorry to see that the calm institutional reserve of these
statements did not extend to the intemperate release issued
by the National Calculating Stockholders' Protest Committee
in the person of its sole surviving officer, Regina Plout. Even
the judicious paraphrasing of the *Times* could not obscure the
tenor of Mrs. Plout's pronouncements: National Calculating
was a hotbed of assassins.

Gloomily Thatcher turned to the other paper. There was
a noticeable air of excitement to its first page. The *Journal*'s
staff very rarely came to grips with a murder, and they were
making the most of their opportunity. Tradition had been
broken, and the story was carried in the upper right-hand
corner. A snappy little article on the future of dehydrated
frozen foods had been mercilessly relegated to page three
while the *Journal* settled down to explain, in suitably con-
fidential tones, the financial and business implications of the
murder. Fortinbras's name did not appear in the headline.

## NATIONAL CALCULATING
## COPES WITH MURDER

### SLAYING AT
### COMPUTER COMPANY

November 8, *Special to the Wall Street Journal:* The computer industry has had to face many problems during the
last five years. These have included customer dissatisfaction
with performance, union resistance to automation, and costly
service difficulties. But National Calculating Company has
been the first to deal with a murder in its offices. Clarence
Fortinbras, leader of the minority shareholder group which
obtained a court order last month to review the books of
National Calculating, was found murdered yesterday afternoon in the home office of that corporation on Madison Avenue. Hard-hitting Charles Mason has steered his computer
company through many shoals since the Korean War but

informed sources on the Street are wondering if Clarence Fortinbras may have won a final victory by the manner of his death.

"I expect the price to slide five to eight points in the next week," said the senior partner of a large brokerage firm, "and I'm advising my customers to unload now." The same advice was being given in other houses. Unless "Chip" Mason can come up with some year-end figures that restore confidence in National Calculating, he can look forward to a rough time at his annual meeting in the spring. Already it is rumored that outside interests are ready to step into Fortinbras's shoes for a proxy battle that will pave the way to a take-over.

"We don't intend to take this lying down," said Mason, a one-time Harvard football great. "Our program will be carried to the stockholders and I know we can count on the support of everybody except the crackpot fringe."

The *Journal* went on to detail possible maneuvers in the hypothetical take-over battle. It was not until the final paragraph that the manner of death was mentioned, and the information on Fortinbras was very skimpy.

Thatcher brushed the papers aside disgustedly. He was sick of the whole mess. Let somebody else worry about it. He drew forward the pile of mail on his desk, selected the items which had been coded by Miss Corsa as requiring his immediate and personal attention, and succeeded in immersing himself in the unsatisfactory condition of the Sloan's relations with its correspondent bank in Albuquerque, New Mexico. So refreshing was this experience that he incautiously accepted a phone call an hour later from Les Thomas, the man at the Sloan who now had the unenviable distinction of keeping an eye on the Bank's investments in National Calculating.

"I'm worried, John. The run has already started."

"Well, so is everybody else who holds National," replied Thatcher sourly.

"You know, John," prodded Thomas anxiously, "the word on the Street is that Fortinbras was about to uncover real dirt."

"It's the word everywhere, Les. We'll just have to grin and bear it."

"But, look, maybe we could . . ."

"Sorry, Les, I've got to run. Have an appointment with Withers," explained Thatcher untruthfully. "Send me a memo!"

Hanging up with a crisp precision that cut off his subordinate's protests, Thatcher decided that, if the world refused to allow him to radiate sweetness and light, he should turn his mind to tasks where a taciturn inflexibility could be used to some profit. To think of inflexibility was to think of Everett Gabler. Thatcher brightened instantly and buzzed for Miss Corsa's presence.

"Memo to Mr. Gabler," he informed her as she poised her pencil over her shorthand book. "And a copy to Mr. Trinkam."

Collecting his thoughts for a moment, he prepared to compose a communication couched in the rolling periods so dear to Everett's heart.

In connection with the disposition and budgetary allocation of Kenneth Nicoll's time, I have reviewed the requirements of your own department and that of Charles Trinkam. You have informed me that the present demands of Mr. Trinkam's department and the irregular calls on Mr. Nicolls have created a situation which is unsatisfactory. As you are aware, the personnel schedule for the forthcoming year has already been approved by the Internal Expenditure Committee and—

As Thatcher settled down to the highly satisfactory task of explaining to Gabler that his, Thatcher's deliberations had resulted in the removal of a man from Gabler's department rather than the hoped-for addition, the phone rang in the suitably muted tones which it assumed in executive offices. Miss Corsa immediately suspended her other activities, and reached for the extension on the side table.

"Good morning. Mr. Thatcher's office. Miss Corsa speaking." There was a subdued roaring noise from the phone.

"Oh, yes, Mr. Robichaux. He's here. Just a moment and I'll put you through."

"Hello . . . John?" bellowed Robichaux amiably.

"Yes?" Thatcher's tone would have deflated most people.

"Say, I just got a call from Chip Mason." Robichaux's tone dropped to an insinuating rumble.

"Bad cess to him."

"Now, John," reproved Robichaux, "Mason's got plenty of troubles right now. It's only right to give him a helping hand."

"Just what did you have in mind, Tom?" Thatcher was genuinely curious. Charitable Robichaux might be in private life. He was certainly not extending a helping hand, *qua* investment banker.

"It's about Cartwright."

Thatcher remained unencouragingly silent.

"You see," confided Tom, "they've still got the police in their ears over at National, and Mason wants Cartwright off the scene. I thought," he suggested cosily, "we might take him to lunch."

"Me go to lunch with Cartwright? Good God, no! Take the General to meet somebody else. It will be a change for him to see someone unconnected with that mess."

"Well, now—"

"No, absolutely not. Good-bye, Tom."

Thatcher turned back to his dictation bitterly. Tom could make a life's work out of succoring Mason if he wanted to. Unless the interests of the Sloan demanded Thatcher's intervention, he would have no further part in it. His thoughts were interrupted by Miss Corsa.

"He's so handsome," she said dreamily.

Thatcher was incredulous.

"Who? Mr. Robichaux?"

"No. General Cartwright."

This was a new aspect of Miss Corsa. Thatcher stared.

"He was on the cover of *Time* magazine," she explained. "He's only forty-seven and a four-star general. He is the chief proponent of conventional armament," she quoted dutifully.

"He is also," Thatcher rejoined, "National Calculating's biggest customer."

Miss Corsa turned back to her book. She was not interested in National Calculating, only in handsome men.

"You were just saying 'As you are aware, the personnel schedule . . .'"

The phone rang.

"Wait a minute," cried Thatcher, arresting Miss Corsa's hand in midair. "I'm out. Gone for the day. You don't know where to reach me. And in order to lend some truthfulness to that statement, I'm going."

He grabbed up his hat and coat and strode to the door followed by Miss Corsa's bemused stare and her sedate tones saying, "Mr. Thatcher's out. Gone for the day."

# 9

# *Alarums and Excursions*

Simply leaving the Sloan Guaranty Trust was not enough to shield John Thatcher from the dislocations caused by the murder of Clarence Fortinbras. Every corner he passed was mined with screaming headlines: "BIZ EXECS QUIZZED," "NAT STOCK COLLAPSE," "EXCHANGE IN UPROAR."

At the corner of Broadway, he hesitated. A moment of reflection was enough to convince him that the University Club, the Bankers Club, and the Harvard Club would be no better. There was the danger of encountering Tom Robichaux, or Francis Devane—or even worse, one of their justly incensed customers. He made a quick calculation: National Calculating Corporation had 500,000 shares outstanding, and, at a guess, 10,000 stockholders. Numbered among that unfortunate group were many of John Thatcher's friends and acquaintances. No, the University Club would not do.

This left him with only one course of action; he would take himself and his briefcase home, pausing only to issue firm directives to the reception desk, and resolutely ignoring the telephone for the rest of the day. Looking really formidable, Thatcher hailed a taxi: a secretary who had been planning to pinch it from beneath his nose took one look at his expression and retreated.

Fortunately, Thatcher's determination to disentangle himself from National Calculating received a powerful assist. In his waiting mail, he found a communication from Consoli-

dated Edison. He extracted the machine-chewed card that
was his bill from an envelope fat with utility whimsy.
("Want to cut winter's chills and bills, Neighbor?") It would
go, via Thatcher's briefcase, to Miss Corsa, who presided
over his bill paying with her customary efficiency. Idly he
glanced at it. There was the usual single chaste line concerning kilowatts. In addition, directly below that line, there
was a block of angular printed information:

CHIBOWA—MOD. 38473859At8
14 ½ elec. v.g. CN 7467

For a moment Thatcher studied this, then he let his eye
drift to the right and downward. "$46.32"

Consolidated Edison was billing him $46.32 for a CHI-
BOWA. He knew, of course, that it was some sort of billing
error. Thatcher's household purchases were effected for him
by a variety of efficient persons connected with the house-
keeping department of the Devonshire, or its Mrs. Anson
who administered the movement of food in and out of his refrigerator, and the transport of goods to and from laundries
and cleaners. If any of these competent and well-paid people
felt that Mr. Thatcher required a $46.32 CHIBOWA, he would
have been presented with what might be termed noncom-
mercial paper; an advertising brochure or a clipping from a
newspaper stapled to a businesslike memorandum beginning:
"To: J. Thatcher, 4B."

But, as he settled himself at his desk and spread the Research Department Preliminary Budget Allocation Study before him—Walter Bowman wanted to hire another statistician
—Thatcher found himself speculating. Mistake or no, what
could a CHIBOWA be?

"Chicken Bone Warmer?" he asked aloud, automatically
putting a question mark next to Walter Bowman's glowing
description of a new publication he was proposing. Like all
Research Departments, the Sloan's thirsted to see itself in
print. Thatcher drew up a memo pad and jotted notes—critical notes—on the subject. At the same time, however, he considered the CHIBOWA. On the whole, Chicken Bone Warmer
seemed unlikely. Chicago-Boston Washer, perhaps.

Now, on the reverse of its much-punched card, Consolidated Edison has thoughtfully tried to spare its patrons just this sort of concern. A telephone number is carefully printed between perforations. Any customer so lost to decency as to question the billing is urged to make use of it.

And the telephone was at John Thatcher's elbow. But as his late wife had frequently pointed out, he had a terrible weakness for puzzles. John Thatcher would no more call Consolidated Edison to learn the precise nature of a CHI-BOWA than he would use a dictionary to solve a crossword puzzle. Briskly composing a riposte to Walter Bowman with one part of his mind, he turned the other part to the CHI-BOWA. A waxer of some sort. Say, a China Bowl Waxer.

Thatcher spent a productive evening without once wondering what the police were uncovering at National Calculating Corporation. After an undisturbed night's sleep, he arrived at the sixth floor of the Sloan the next morning, in the best of spirits.

"No, I'll read the papers later, Miss Corsa." The papers, he already knew, were screaming that the police were pressing their investigation of the murder of Clarence Fortinbras. And no more. "And, Miss Corsa, send Bowman a list of every publication that emanates from this bank. No, nothing else, just the list. And I'll be busy for the next half-hour . . . er, private business."

He had the grace to feel guilty when the door shut behind her. It was Miss Corsa's task and pleasure to deal with such outsiders as Consolidated Edison (except, of course, when it was a question of bond issues or annual meetings). But if Miss Corsa dealt with the billing error, John Thatcher might remain unenlightened about the CHIBOWA. He had bet himself ten dollars that it was a China Bowl Waxer, and another five dollars that he could find this out without direct inquiry. Loss meant donation to the Salvation Army.

Drawing out the bill, he dialed. (And in her office, Miss Corsa looked at the green light on her phone with disapproval. It was never a good sign when Mr. Thatcher did his own dialing.)

Thatcher first reached a voice inquiring about his needs.

No sooner had he mentioned the word "bill" than he was routed forward.

"Good morning! This is Miss Goodfellow. How may I help you?" The voice could be described only as seductive.

"Well, you see . . ."

Miss Goodfellow broke in to plead. "Could I have your name and address?"

Thatcher supplied them.

"Thank you," Miss Goodfellow breathed warmly. "Now, would you mind waiting just for a second?"

There was a pause during which Miss Goodfellow consulted a file. At her return, Thatcher began, "I have received a bill . . ."

"Oh, I do so hope you have it there with you," said Miss Goodfellow. "It makes everything so much easier."

Thatcher admitted that he did have his bill before him.

"Good. Now, just what is our trouble?"

Speaking carefully, Thatcher pointed out that he had been billed $46.32 by error. He added that he would appreciate rectification, then waited hopefully.

Miss Goodfellow gave vent to little cries of distress, then again retreated to her files. When she returned there was a merry bubble in her voice.

"I see that our records do show delivery of this item, Mr. Thatcher. But do you know what I think? I think that Mrs. Thatcher ordered it, and forgot to tell hubby. Don't you think that's a possibility?"

"I do not," said Thatcher quellingly, but Miss Goodfellow swept on.

"After all, how many mornings do you go into the kitchen to watch Baby's food being prepared?"

Thatcher removed the receiver from his ear and stared at it. Getting competent help is not easy, but surely Consolidated Edison was not . . . Miss Goodfellow was still speaking.

"So, what do those doctors know! Cold food! Why, I was really shocked! When you think of how a good hot meal feels! That's why the Child's Bottle Warmer is such a popular product. And Mr. Thatcher, believe me, you will find it well worth the money . . ."

Thatcher stabbed the button for Miss Corsa. "Just one minute, Miss Goodfellow. . . . Miss Corsa, will you please handle this?" He handed her Con Ed's bill. "They're trying to charge me for a bottle warmer."

Miss Corsa clucked and returned to her desk just as Charlie Trinkam sauntered past her into his chief's office. "Bottle warmers? Oh, hot rum toddies. Well, put those pleasant thoughts from your mind, John, and brace yourself. The Exchange has just suspended trading in National Calculating. All hell is breaking loose."

Trinkam was perfectly accurate. Murder normally unleashes a whirlwind of activity: police inquiries into the whereabouts of interested parties, meticulous examinations of the premises where the body was found, interviews with relatives and acquaintances. But murder in a large corporation has financial overtones. Even as the New York City Police Department was pursuing its massive attempt to discover who murdered Clarence Fortinbras, the New York financial community began its efforts to keep National Calculating Corporation from becoming the second victim.

Before Miss Corsa had finished bringing Consolidated Edison to its senses, Bradford Withers, president of the Sloan Guaranty Trust, hurried down from his penthouse office to reveal that he had been receiving urgent telephone calls.

"From Mason, and from Frank Devane," he said portentously. "And old Mike Perkins, and Fletcher, over at Asprey Brothers. . . ."

Since this enumeration could continue indefinitely, Thatcher interrupted to ask what the callers wanted.

Withers shot his cuffs. "The general feeling, as I gather it, John, is that perhaps there is something that the Sloan and other interested parties can do to shore up National during this storm."

"Yes?" said Thatcher cautiously while Charlie Trinkam, a participant in the conference, frowned.

"I told Devane to get in touch with you," Withers continued. "We'll want to do what we can, of course."

This pronouncement was a figure of speech. Withers, having given the Sloan the benefit of his executive decision, immediately departed for a long weekend in Shaftesbury, Connecticut, leaving his staff to attend to the details.

They were many; conferences, telephone calls, and appointments—between the Sloan, Robichaux and Devane, large numbers of lawyers, two members of the Board of Governors of the New York Stock Exchange, and several Board members from National Calculating. All these parties gathered at a culminating session late Sunday night, held at Robichaux's Long Island home to elude the press which was having a field day with National's secretarial staff and with accountants who did not want to be quoted. (If the police were making any progress, they were keeping it from the newspaper-reading public.) Since Robichaux's estate on the North Shore was conspicuously inaccessible, and since not a single man sitting in the timbered library was in his first youth, the whole conclave reminded John Thatcher of an eccentric memorial for a departed friend.

Nevertheless, business was transacted. It was decided that Clarence Fortinbras's audit should continue, under the aegis of the Sloan Guaranty Trust and Robichaux and Devane, representing the several interested parties.

"That way we'll restore confidence in the stock," said the man from the Stock Exchange.

His exhausted companions looked at him.

"Well, it can't hurt," he countered defensively.

Chip Mason roused himself from his stupor. Staring resentfully at the glass of milk (on a silver salver) just handed him by the houseboy, he protested. National Calculating had nothing to hide, but they had the police in and out of every office, asking people damned fool questions, questions like where had they gone to lunch on Wednesday, when had they last seen Clarence Fortinbras. The last thing National Calculating needed was more outsiders asking more questions. His board members exchanged looks and spoke peremptorily. Looking fretful, Mason subsided.

Tom Robichaux, splendid in a preposterous smoking jacket, took pity on him. With an expansive wave of his glass

he said, "Now listen, Chip, it's got to be. But I can see that
you're worried about breaking it to your people, so I'll tell
you what we'll do. John and I will come down first thing in
the morning. We'll have a little front office meeting, and
put it on the line to them . . ."

There was a general murmur of approval from the assembly, but Chip Mason did not look particularly grateful,
Thatcher thought. He himself was resigned. Robichaux, however, was smiling genially as he accompanied those of his
guests who were departing to their transport. At the door,
he turned to urge his house guests to make free with night-
caps.

The man from the Stock Exchange took him at his word.
"Just a short one, Thatcher? No? Probably you're right. Look
at what late hours and brandy have done to poor old Tom.
I've always maintained that that explains . . ." He coughed
and broke off. "Still, I'm glad that you'll be sitting in on that
meeting tomorrow."

"You mean better me than you?" Thatcher replied.

"Exactly," said the Stock Exchange man candidly.

His frankness proved justified. By Monday morning, Tom
Robichaux's Napoleonic phase was over. But, as he told
Thatcher on the interminable drive from Long Island to the
Southern Bourbon Building, somebody had to crack the whip
at National Calculating.

"Somebody has," Thatcher pointed out acidly.

"I'll just lay it on the line," said Robichaux resolutely.

This he did as soon as he and Thatcher had been ushered
into the sixteenth-floor conference room where Charles
Mason and his associates waited. National Calculating was
not greeting its distinguished visitors warmly, Thatcher saw
as he took his place at the table, but despite the almost pal-
pable atmosphere of tension, Robichaux proceeded to deliver
himself of a brief homily centering on the financial reper-
cussions of Clarence Fortinbras's murder, and the consequent
need for a continuation of the audit. He could not complain
that his audience was unresponsive.

"I don't like it. We're being thrown to the wolves!" Harry

Blaney's voice was perilously close to hysteria, and there was an uneasy stir in the room.

Robichaux was vexed. "But we're not throwing anybody to the wolves. That's the point! We want to protect National Calculating . . ."

"As much as we legitimately can," Thatcher interposed smoothly. This produced appraisal from Jay Rutledge, who was sitting next to him, then depressed silence.

Robichaux looked around. "Does anybody else have any objections?"

From the far end of the table, Morris Richter spoke. "Why should we? For God's sake, it's perfectly clear that we're all in a mess. Fortinbras was killed while he was going over the books. Our only defense is to insist that somebody continue that audit, otherwise we're all under a cloud, and not in the stock market! God knows what the police are going to come up with!"

Harry Blaney, sitting across the table, drew his mouth into a derisive smile. Allen Hammond frowned at Richter. Richter himself simply glared. Discovering Clarence Fortinbras's body had shaken him, as had the discovery that the New York City Police Department questions everybody, including brilliant scientists. Belatedly, and under trying circumstances, he was growing up.

"Well?" he demanded challengingly.

"I think you're right," said Mrs. Cobb in an emotionless voice. Looking straight at Harry Blaney, she added, "What else can we do?"

Thatcher studied Mrs. Cobb for a moment. She seemed in control of herself, but he heard a constricted note in her voice. The murder of Clarence Fortinbras had touched everybody at National.

Harry Blaney scowled. "My God! Another audit? Do you have any idea of what that means? Fortinbras turned the whole division upside down. Snatched files, grabbed secretaries. He was going out to the Jersey plant to take a physical inventory! He would have put production back by at least 20 percent . . ."

"All right!" Thatcher snapped as Blaney's voice mounted

into a reedy chant. "Chip has already told us that Fortinbras went too far. He was probably human enough to react to your hostility . . ."

"Hostility!" Chip Mason squeaked while a murmur of protest went around the table. "What do you expect? We tried to remain courteous, but that man made it impossible!"

"Chip," said Thatcher wearily, "why don't you all forget your complaints about Clarence Fortinbras, and concentrate on the current dilemma?"

This produced another depressed silence. Blaney was saying something under his breath. Allen Hammond, Mrs. Cobb, and Jay Rutledge had retreated into their own thoughts. Morris Richter hated the world. Chip Mason was near tears.

Thatcher was irritated by all this self-pity. Moreover, he had rather liked Clarence Fortinbras. "Remember that the police will demand an official audit. If we're already proceeding with one, they may . . . er, modify the rigors of their own investigation."

The good sense of this observation was not without effect, but instinctively his co-workers waited for Harry Blaney's response.

He looked up. "Sure. O.K. If it's going to be, it's going to be. But I want to register a protest at the way the ball is bouncing around here!"

"Now, Harry," Mason began.

Blaney, consulting his watch, shrugged insubordinately. "I've got an important meeting." He was on his feet and striding to the door. Just before he left the room, he said, "I'll cooperate." Then they could hear him pounding down the hall.

Jay Rutledge chose his words with care. "Commercial Sales bore the brunt of Fortinbras. That's why Harry is so mad about this new audit."

Thatcher looked at him thoughtfully, but Robichaux was more receptive. "Don't blame him," he said simply. "Now, are there any more objections, or will the rest of you cooperate? I think I can promise you that we won't be as disruptive as Fortinbras was."

There was a confused murmur of assent.

"Still don't like it," Mason muttered. "Letting Harry down . . ."

Mrs. Cobb cut in like a ruthless schoolmistress. "It isn't a question of letting Harry down, Charles. It's a question of simple survival. We have to go along."

Again, Jay Rutledge added his support. "I'm willing to cooperate with a normal businesslike audit," he said. "Always have been."

Allen Hammond promised cooperation insofar as his cooperation was called for. Morris Richter shrugged to indicate that any alternative was unthinkable. The meeting was over.

Charles Mason was so doleful that his nephew was moved to a rare touch of sympathy. "Cheer up, Uncle Chas," he said. "We'll come through. There's always General Cartwright."

Mason brightened faintly and turned to Rutledge who was just rising to leave. "Sure. This ruckus didn't help," he said, "but we turn out a mighty good piece of work. And Cartwright knows it. Unless something else happens . . ."

Tom Robichaux was beautifully blunt. "Well, for God's sake, let's see that nothing else does happen!"

They left Mason relapsed into gloom.

Thatcher taxied back to Wall Street with Robichaux.

"We'll send Addison in tomorrow," he said reminding himself to tell Miss Corsa that he wanted to talk to the Sloan's accountant before he went to National.

"Fine," said Robichaux absently. "That press release can go out this afternoon, then. Well, we've done what we can." He paused, then added, "What a bunch! What did you think?"

Thatcher tugged at an earlobe and compromised on evasion. "They weren't at their best, of course."

Robichaux's financial commitments disposed him to grasp at straws. "Still, as Rutledge said, they've got a good product. And Government Contracts Division is first-rate . . ."

"Mmm," said Thatcher. "Well, if we've convinced that first-rate division and all the rest of them to try to get on with their work, we'll have made a significant contribution to National Calculating."

# 10

# *Thrift, Thrift, Horatio!*

At National Calculating Corporation, the work did go on, considerably hampered by the cyclonic activities connected with Clarence Fortinbras's murder, and interrupted by inconvenient queries from the New York City Police Department, the press, and every brokerage house in the country. "This is the time," said the Memorandum to Staff (Executive and Support) "to put our shoulders to the wheel and march down the field." The author of this rallying cry then resisted the temptation to take his milk and Gelusil in the tranquillity of Westport, and indeed surpassed himself in the number of forays he made, chiefly into the Law Department.

"Nobody can say that old Chip doesn't have grit," Kellog said ruminatively to one of his subordinates.

"But is grit enough?" his junior replied.

Happily, the terrifying spectacle of National's president resolutely trying to radiate confident strength was not visited on most of his staff, who were all fully occupied by their own difficulties. Jay Rutledge, thinner and more hatchetlike than ever, could be seen tirelessly ushering General Cartwright in and out of Government Contracts Division while his staff produced a whole literature on the TCR. Morris Richter, ferocious with resolution, abandoned casual charm, and retreated into the recesses of the Research and Development Division to tyrannize his underlings with cold comments on projects-in-process. Mrs. Cobb grimly soothed ruffled scientific sensibilities.

Harry Blaney plunged in and out of the Commercial Sales Division with unpredictable speed, alternating open savagery with sudden moods of wistfulness that reduced his secretary to complete helplessness.

In the Public Relations Department, Andrew L. Andrews drafted seven versions of "A Letter to Our Stockholders," one hundred and thirty-two press releases, and went without sleep for five consecutive nights, at the end of which period he collapsed in exhaustion, and was removed on a stretcher, exciting considerable alarm in the elevator as he was borne away.

There was much activity among the secretarial staff concerning floral offerings to the bereaved Mrs. Fortinbras.

Local 747, United Electrical Workers of America, staged a wildcat protest strike in Elkhart, Indiana, and since nobody was very clear what they were protesting, the Controller felt that it was his duty to prolong his absence from the home office, thus confirming his colleagues' suspicion that he had an abnormally keen instinct for self-preservation.

Miss Quackenbush, the office manager, chose this period to institute a new supply room control system, designed to cut down the pilfering of ball-point pens, and created so complex a procedure that for several days it was impossible to obtain any carbon paper without requisitioning it on seven carbons, a self-defeating aspect of the scheme that had escaped her.

In short, National Calculating was a hive of brisk stridings, muted clackings, and demonic dictations, all conveying to the uninitiated the impression that the show was going on with its usual efficiency.

There was just one small pool of repose.

Sitting in one corner of the Accounting Department (fifteenth floor) on Wednesday morning, untouched by the bursts of activity eddying around them, sat three men calmly drinking their morning coffee, not from paper cups but from china mugs produced as a token of respect and cooperation by the sixteenth floor. They moved with unhurried self-assurance (or at least two of them did) and spoke with the elliptic, low-voiced portentousness of surgeons conferring at a particularly interesting incision.

They were the accountants: Henry Addison, detailed from the Sloan Guaranty Trust to continue Fortinbras's work on behalf of the Bank and Robichaux and Devane; Fred Cohen, representing the New York City Police Department, who had arrived on Addison's heels the day before; and again detailed to provide, aid, comfort, and what assistance he could, young Stanley Draper, whose first-hand knowledge of notable accountants were being considerably enlarged at the expense of his mastery of the intricacies of Petty Cash and Expense Accounts.

Punctilious politeness was the order of the day where lesser men might have found some awkwardness. Mr. Cohen, who had the authority of Authority behind him, had not needed instructions from above to offer complete cooperation with Mr. Addison; Mr. Addison, representing the Sloan (a not insignificant contributor to the Police Athletic League) was personally delighted to comply with Mr. Thatcher's instructions to cooperate with the police. The specialists entered into a completely satisfactory division of labor at once, united by their common interest in the ways in which quite clever people make mistakes. On paper.

"Of course, I haven't had your opportunity to do a lot of that sort of work," Addison said generously.

Cohen made a pleased noise. In cooperation with certain Federal authorities, he had just effected the deportation of a surprised New Yorker who, if he was the beer salesman he claimed, had been able to afford some startlingly high-priced legal talent.

"You'd think that Capone would have taught all of these people a lesson," Stanley said naïvely.

The remark pleased the older man. "Oh, they're careful," Cohen said with a comfortable laugh. "But not careful enough for us. For example, when we came across that deferred interest charge, we knew we had him. It was just a question of finding out where he'd deposited his bonds."

"Very, very nice," said Addison. It was the tribute of one master to another.

Neither Addison nor Cohen was of the Fortinbras breed. Perhaps because they were not academics, they lacked his high vocalism. On the contrary, they were both notably sparing of words, and Stanley, who had spent a hopeful Tuesday with them pointing out Mr. Fortinbras's accumulation, and Wednesday morning showing them Commercial Sales' current files, had not yet heard any dicta. Naturally, he was grateful for the opportunity to observe such noted practioners of his art, but he felt slightly disappointed.

"Interesting," Mr. Addison would comment, handing Mr. Cohen a clutch of canceled checks.

Cohen would flip through them, frown, and jot down a few figures. "I see what you mean."

An ambitious young man could learn little from this except by confessing total confusion. Stanley could not complain that either man lacked courtesy in spelling out his conclusions upon request, but it was apparent that they lacked Clarence Fortinbras's pedagogic zeal.

Stanley harbored the uncomfortable impression that if he had not known Clarence Fortinbras, Mr. Addison and Mr. Cohen would be treating him as no more than a junior official in the Accounting Department, in charge of Petty Cash and Expense Accounts.

But neither of them had been acquainted with Clarence Fortinbras, and they were naturally interested in what Stanley so artlessly told them about the dean of accounting. The more so, as he had been found with the cord of his own adding machine wrapped around his neck.

"I never thought that being an accountant was a particularly dangerous profession," Fred Cohen remarked, shifting easily. He was a steady worker when he worked, and a complete relaxer when he relaxed. "Tony Panelli shot at me once, but that was during Prohibition, and I've always maintained he was aiming at Captain Pettley. That's who he got, anyway."

"How could Fortinbras have been killed that way?" Addison wanted to know.

As befits a man on the staff of the Police Department, Cohen was knowledgeable. "Well," he said, absentmindedly pouring himself another cup of coffee, "it would have been fairly easy. If somebody was, say, peering over his shoulder, they could have looped that cord around his neck in just a minute . . ."

"Wouldn't he shout? Or fight back. I should think it would take a really strong man to do it."

"No," Cohen said authoritatively. "Remember, he was an old man. The shock would probably immobilize him. And of course he couldn't make a noise with that cord biting into his neck. He'd probably just sag, then it would be a question of finishing the job in a minute or two . . ."

Stanley was chilled.

"Of course he was flamboyant," Addison commented thoughtfully. "First-rate man but flamboyant methods." His tone suggested that Clarence Fortinbras's surprising death was not altogether out of keeping with his daring methods of cost accounting.

"Let's hope that nobody around here is a compulsive accountant killer."

"Do you think that there's any danger?" Stanley could not keep from demanding. He was wide-eyed, not with fright, but with the thrill of living dangerously.

"No."

"Do the police . . .?"

"I don't know what the police think," Cohen said so smoothly that it was obvious it was a much-used formula. "I'm just an accountant."

Stanley flushed, and Addison took pity on him. "You have an interesting set-up here," he said kindly. "I've been running up some inventory estimates for Commercial Sales this morning, and comparing them with what the Controller's office has from Government Sales."

"That isn't much, is it? I don't think we're going to find much about Government Sales until we move into it."

"Mr. Rutledge presents an independent summary," Stanley explained. "It's incorporated into the financial report, of course, but the running summaries are prepared in his office.

That's why the Controller won't have much information from Government Contracts until the six months' statement is being prepared."

"Yes," Addison said. He had already ascertained all this and more, but he wanted to encourage Stanley. "It's got some justification because keeping the most profitable division clear means that you do show up any weaknesses in Commercial Sales, as well as Research and Development, but I'm not convinced that it's the soundest accounting practice."

"Well, I talked to Harry Blaney yesterday," said Cohen lazily, "and as far as I can see, he's reason enough to explain why Commercial Sales is doing badly. I needn't say, Stanley, that this is in confidence?"

Absently Stanley assured Cohen that he would not repeat the indiscretion. His attention had wandered to a slight problem of his own. The fiscal month was drawing to a close, and it was time for him to present the totals on Petty Cash and Expense Accounts. And he still hadn't got Mrs. Cobb's statement or cleared up that luncheon bill with Mr. Rutledge. What would these men say if they knew how he was letting his own work slide in the excitement of recent events! It was time he buckled down and put his own house into that apple-pie order so highly recommended by Clarence Fortinbras.

"I think I'll go down to my office, if you gentlemen don't need me," he suggested.

They watched him go.

"Nice boy," Cohen remarked.

"Mmm," Addison agreed. With Stanley's departure, he was not indisposed for a spot of professional gossip.

"Did he tell you about the fuss Fortinbras raised?"

"Fuss?" asked Cohen innocently. Actually, Stanley had told them both, but Cohen was by nature cautious.

"About Fortinbras's story that somebody stole papers from his office." Addison explained. He did not resent Cohen's caution but respected it.

A short silence reigned.

"I don't think that there's much doubt that somebody did loot that office," Addison said, after a pause. "I've been checking through the records for Commercial Sales. Unless I'm mistaken"—and Cohen smiled at this absurdity—"unless I'm mistaken, several months' records are missing. And I've already seen Fortinbras's rough outline. He had them when he started working. That means the papers were in that office at one time. They aren't there now."

"That's interesting," Cohen said quietly. "There are some big gaps in the Expense Accounts too. I have a feeling that we'll find other holes as we go on. But we won't know about that for a few days."

"It's a funny combination of papers to be missing."

Another thoughtful pause.

"I suppose it's possible that Fortinbras took them home to work on. I don't see why . . ."

"Fortinbras didn't take any papers home," Cohen said. "Lieutenant Cortell checked. I think I'll just mention this to him. Of course we'll have to tell Mason too."

"And if you don't have any objection," Addison replied courteously, "I think I'll report that fact to Mr. Thatcher. At the moment, I don't see any sense in stealing these items, but it's interesting. It does confirm Fortinbras's claims."

"Shows how innocent some people are," said Cohen with a chuckle. "As if any of them could have kept Fortinbras from finding what he wanted."

The accountants smiled grimly.

Then they got back to work, pausing only to dictate a joint memorandum to Charles Mason on the subject of missing financial records.

This document, arriving at the presidential office not many hours later, merely added to the prevailing gloom. In his own quarters, Mason abandoned his public aplomb for profound self-pity. He read the memorandum with lackluster eye.

"What can I do about this?" he demanded querulously. "I'm about at the end of my tether."

Mary Sullivan, much tried during the past few days and fresh from an irritating encounter with Allen Hammond, bit back the retort that sprang to mind about the shortness of Mr. Mason's tether.

Thatcher expelled his breath softly as Addison came to the end of his report. "There's no doubt about this, I take it?"

Addison shook his head. "No. Of course, we can't make a complete schedule of what's missing. But there's no doubt that somebody got his hands on Fortinbras's material. Exactly as he claimed."

"Is this going to hold you up?"

"No. We won't be able to tell exactly what's been taken until we finish the audit. Even then we won't know for sure."

Thatcher rubbed his jaw for a moment. Then he asked: "What about the scene that Fortinbras made after the looting? Did he mention anything specific?"

"It's hard to find out without making inquiries," Addison replied. "All Cohen and I have heard is the general gossip. Draper—that's the boy who was helping Fortinbras—might be able to help us. But we didn't want to make this public until you and Lieutenant Cortell had been filled in."

Thatcher nodded hasty agreement. "Of course not. You say you sent a memo to Mason. Well, he won't be able to help, but some of the others might remember something."

"I don't know," said Addison doubtfully. "The way I heard it, they more or less drifted in piecemeal. Richter and Hammond came back in the middle of the row, Blaney just walked out on the whole business, and Rutledge was entertaining General Cartwright so he missed the fight. I tell you what, though. Miss Sullivan was there and frankly—" Addison paused delicately.

Thatcher grinned at this unspoken commentary on the front office of National Calculating. "You think she has more sense than the rest of them put together?"

"Well, one thing's sure. She's likely to have been more detached than anyone else there. As I understand it, everybody else went right up into the air at the mere suggestion that someone had stolen a bunch of papers. Nobody paid much attention to the details of Fortinbras's complaint. But she might remember if he mentioned anything specific."

Thatcher was inclined to agree with Addison. He made a

mental note to have a quiet word with Mary Sullivan. In the meantime, he turned his attention to the tentative list the accountants had prepared.

"It doesn't seem to make much sense, does it? Commercial Sales Records and then some Expense Account items."

"No, it doesn't. Particularly as Cohen and I got the impression that there are other gaps too—some capital improvement items from Research, and some cost items from Government Contracts. Of course, expense accounts are always tricky when a full-scale investigation starts."

Thatcher snorted. "It would take more than a little juggling of expense accounts to explain the situation at that company." He paused for a moment. "But you're right, somebody may have gone into a panic about some minor padding after Fortinbras was killed. I take it that's what you're suggesting?"

Addison smiled. "Precisely."

"Well, I think we can safely let Robichaux talk to Mason about this." He buzzed his intercom, and within seconds Miss Corsa was busy with the switchboard at Robichaux and Devane.

Tom Robichaux was only too willing to talk to Chip Mason about this latest evidence of skulduggery at National. His tone of voice, irresistibly suggestive of a testy hippopotamus to Thatcher, evoked a more powerful image to Chip Mason not many minutes later. A lion balked of his prey, for instance.

"Now Tom . . . Yes, I know, I've just seen that memo from those damned accountants . . . What's that? . . . You can't do this to us. It'll crucify us . . . Just a few little expense account items . . . Please, Tom, for old times sake. . . ."

Putting her receiver noiselessly back on its cradle, Mary Sullivan considered the incredible oddity of the masculine character. Then, with a sigh, she went to the refrigerator in the closet. Now, if ever, was the time for milk.

# 11

# Distant Revelry

Chip Mason did not plead in vain. As a result, given Tom Robichaux's highly idiosyncratic system of logic, John Putnam Thatcher found himself, late that evening hunched in the corner of a taxicab bearing him swiftly to the Greenwich Village apartment of Morris Richter. He surveyed his companion with exasperation. What idiot idea had possessed Robichaux? To decide to descend on Richter unannounced and question him about the missing expense accounts! In the middle of the night too. Thatcher sighed heavily. It was all the fault of old Barnwell at Barnwell and McBridge. They might be good lawyers, but they were not realists. On second thought, Thatcher, always fair-minded, admitted to himself that they must be good lawyers—considering the number of divorces from which Tom had emerged relatively unscathed. No, the real trouble was Tom. Deprived of wifely consortium and debarred from forbidden fruit, he was at a loss for social occupation. Come to think of it, one always did see a lot of him during these periods of adjustment.

The taxi came to a halt on Christopher Street before a remodeled brownstone from which sounds of music and laughter emanated.

"Well," said Robichaux cheerily, "It looks as if we've stumbled onto a party."

"This is absurd," said Thatcher tartly. "We can't go up

and question the man about National Calculating if he's entertaining."

Robichaux instantly paid the cabbie, and waved him away briskly. "Now that's where you're wrong, John," he said persuasively. "We couldn't ask for anything better. Perfect cover, you know." He halted under the streetlamp and stared owlishly down at Thatcher. "Everyone will think we're guests."

"Bah! What do you think we are, Tom? OSS men in Casablanca? We're here to ask the man a few simple questions which anyone in his right mind would do tomorrow morning in the office."

Robichaux's coaxing hand steered him into the lobby of the building. "But it's not as if we were deliberately intruding. Mason's asked us to have a talk with Richter, and the other Division Managers, so we've come here where we can be private. Of course, if Richter finds it inconvenient to see us right now, why then we . . . Er—" here Robichaux sketched an airy gesture, "Why, we'll just leave, that's all," he concluded triumphantly.

"Very handsome of us." In spite of himself, Thatcher laughed. "You mean we won't put him to the trouble of throwing us out forcibly. You know, Tom, it would serve you right if he did just that."

But Thatcher's hopes died stillborn. Morris Richter, although surprised, was apparently delighted to see them.

"Come in, come in," he invited. "What's that? Something about National Calculating? Yes, of course. But first let me get you a drink. Josie and I are having some friends from Columbia in for the evening." Richter's voice was raised in a genial shout to penetrate the din which had accompanied him to the doorway. "Just pile your coats on the chest and join the crowd. I won't be a minute."

Their host disappeared through an archway to the right of the entrance hall while the two men obeyed his instructions.

"You know," said Thatcher, lowering his voice to a sibilant whisper, "I can't decide whether he's just buttering up the Sloan as a matter of principle or whether he's really too dewy-eyed to realize that our being here is quite extraordinary."

"Neither," said Robichaux firmly, "He's simply giving a party."

Upon reflection, Thatcher was inclined to agree. From the little he had seen, Richter was still young enough to be constantly assuming poses of one sort or another. Tonight he was playing the part of host, and his actions automatically adjusted to the role. If two firemen axed their way through the front door bearing a large hose, Richter would greet them with cries of enthusiasm and offers of refreshment.

Thatcher paused to take stock of his surroundings. Robichaux and he were standing on the threshhold of a high-ceilinged room which was enormous by present-day standards. All details, however, were obliterated by a solid wall of humanity which was standing, smoking, laughing, drinking, screeching, and—yes, by heaven—even singing it appeared. He taxed their host with the last phenomenon upon his reappearance carrying two glasses of brandy.

"Georgi," replied Richter with dignity, "is singing Albanian folk songs."

"Indeed," murmured Thatcher politely.

Richter warmed to his subject. "There's quite a fad for them now. You may not know it, but—"

Thatcher interrupted firmly. He had not come here to be instructed about quaint Balkan customs. "Indeed I do. A very interesting field, I have long felt."

"Well then, you'll want to meet Georgi. Just a second. It'll be easier if I bring him," said Richter, plunging once again into the mob.

"Albanian folk songs!"

"What's that?" Robichaux was sipping his brandy thoughtfully. "Not bad at all," he summed up judiciously. "Usually at an artsy-craftsy shindig like this, you're lucky not to get some hellish punch."

Thatcher was frankly incredulous. "Oh, come off it, Tom. When was the last time you were at a party like this? When you were young and innocent?"

"Now, there's where you're wrong," said Robichaux without heat. "It was when I was still with Helena." He paused reminiscently. "She was interested in literature."

"Here we are!" Richter had reemerged, accompanied by two striking figures. "This is Georgi Borof, who sings." He clapped an affectionate hand on the shoulder of a hulking, bearded giant, whose left hand engulfed an absurdly fragile balalaika. "And this is Katrina Tametz, who records for Folkways. Katrina, this is John Thatcher and Tom Robichaux."

Built on generous lines, Katrina was deep-bosomed and long-legged, with a mass of Titian-colored hair in the midst of which gleamed long copper earrings as she turned her head to follow the introductions. She favored Robichaux with a long, thoughtful gaze. He brightened instantly.

"My songs, they are simple but very beautiful," said Georgi, addressing himself to Thatcher. "I sing of our mountains, our rocks and our Skanderbeg." He sighed deeply.

"Er—quite so."

"It is very sad to an Albanian to be distant from his home. When I am sad, I sing. Presently I shall sing for you."

"That will be delightful," said Thatcher, dismayed. Morris Richter hovered nearby, watching indulgently much as a parent watches the beginning of a nice children's party.

"But first," said Georgi suggestively, "in order to sing, I must drink. It is always so."

"Of course," soothed Richter. "Just help yourself. You know where the bar is."

"I go now, but I shall return," Georgi promised Thatcher, making him a deep and unsteady bow. "You are of those who have the soul to appreciate."

"You've made a great hit with Georgi," congratulated Richter. "He doesn't take to many people."

"Now, listen, Richter," said Thatcher, a note of desperation in his voice, "I don't want to butt in on your party. There are just a few questions. It won't take a minute. Perhaps we could go somewhere—" Thatcher looked helplessly about him.

"Afraid the party's flowed into every room," replied

Richter proudly, "but nobody will take any notice of us here."

"Very well. Mason has asked Robichaux and me to try and find out a few things quietly. Tom—" Thatcher looked over his shoulder. Robichaux had disappeared. He continued resignedly. "The point is, the accountants have discovered that a batch of papers are missing from Fortinbras's files."

Richter whistled softly. Thatcher was relieved to find that the young man appreciated the situation without elaboration. After a few days of dealing with Mason, Thatcher had begun to develop an explanatory technique which bordered on the offensive. He went on to outline the absence of expense account vouchers and Mason's belief that this was no more than a cover for routine padding.

"Absolute nonsense," said Richter with surprising firmness.

"What's absolute nonsense?" asked a jovial voice. Robichaux had returned, hospitably bearing a tray of drinks and still accompanied by Katrina Tametz, who was laughing richly. She had very white teeth.

"This business about somebody stealing the expense account records." Richter seemed to have no objection to discussing National's business in front of Katrina. Absentmindedly, he helped himself from the tray. "First of all, National isn't a very lavish firm. Oh, there's the usual company joyriding. Junkets to San Francisco and that sort of thing. But as far as European trips, yachts, estates on Long Island Sound—well, there isn't anything of that magnitude. Secondly, if there were, it wouldn't do any good to hook the papers. Stanley Draper would still know all about it. You know Draper? He's the accountant in charge of expenses. And he's got an indelible memory." An old grievance absorbed Richter's attention for a moment. "Do you know he tried to tackle me once about taxi fares to New Jersey. Said it would be cheaper to use a company car! Little squirt."

"Well, he sounds conscientious, anyway. He certainly ought to remember anything really big."

"Come to think of it, Draper should be well worth ques-

tioning. You know he's got the office next to the one where
Fortinbras was working. I remember now that when Fortinbras was making all that fuss about stolen papers—and it
looks as if he was right, doesn't it?—Draper was dancing
around, making a fool of himself. Wouldn't be surprised if
he was in his office while the murder was being committed.
And to do him justice," said Richter with the air of one giving the devil his due, "he notices a hell of a lot. Not what
you really want in somebody who's handling executive expense accounts. It needs a little tact. But he might be useful
from your point of view."

"You're right," said Thatcher. "Draper seems to have been
strangely overlooked. For that matter, so has Mrs. Cobb."

"What about Mrs. Cobb?" asked Richter sharply.

"I don't see where she fits into the picture," remarked
Thatcher mildly.

"Dr. Cobb is assistant manager of the Research and Development Division. She is an extremely able executive and
a distinguished scientist." Richter's voice ended on a distinct
snap.

Thatcher raised his eyebrows. "I'm sure she is. That isn't
exactly what I had in mind. I meant her position in this
whole Fortinbras affair. Did she resist his invasion of the
company the way everybody else did? I couldn't help notic-
ing at our meeting the other day that, while she was very
reserved, she was also very upset."

"Naturally she was upset." Richter flushed with annoy-
ance. "It's enough to make anybody—"

But a new entrant joined the conversation. "This woman,
she is a scientist? That is very unwomanly." Katrina Tametz
brooded disapprovingly for a moment, then smiled confi-
dingly up at Robichaux. "Me, I am very womanly!"

"Good for you," said Robichaux enthusiastically.

"Josie! Come here and meet some people," called Richter,
capitalizing on the interruption.

A small, wiry woman detached herself from a group of
people gathered around a bespectacled youth reading from
a crumpled manuscript. She was wearing a black leotard

covered by a sleeveless and full-flowing smock striped in orange and yellow. Introductions followed.

"Oh, yes, Mr. Thatcher," she chirped, "Georgi has told me all about you. How interesting that you should be an expert on Balkan folk songs."

Thatcher eyed her with misgivings. "Oh, it's nothing at all," he said modestly.

"We need some refills here, Josie. I'll get them."

"Wait, Morrie. I'll come with you. I had to borrow some ice. We're running out." She skipped off at the side of her husband.

Robichaux chuckled. "Saved by the bell, John. I bet she's got a Serb poet somewhere you ought to meet."

"What a perfectly extraordinary garment," said Thatcher weakly.

Robichaux hugged Katrina affectionately. "Very unwomanly," he said disapprovingly.

"No," said Katrina surprisingly. "She is right. If you have a figure not at all, then it is best to shroud the body in mystery."

There was a dampened silence until Richter returned. Thatcher took up the conversation instantly. He had a feeling that Time's winged chariot, in the form of a Serb poet, was pressing at his heels.

"You know, Richter," he said significantly, "since the confirmation of Fortinbras's ideas about stolen papers, the police are working on the theory that criminal fraud, rather than sheer ineptitude, is responsible for the bad showing at National."

Richter considered the possibility dispassionately. The idea was obviously not new to him. "Very probable," he said quietly. "After all, people don't commit murder without a strong motive. But you have to approach this thing logically. The basic situation is very simple. When you talk about the 'bad showing' at National, you mean the net profits are too low. Now," he said, warming to his theme and allowing a professorial tone to swell his volume, "what are net profits? They are a figure in a very simple equation."

He paused dramatically and took a refreshing sip from his glass.

It occurred to Thatcher that everybody was slightly drunk. He himself was still abstemiously consuming his first glass of brandy. But Richter and Robichaux, in a smooth, businesslike manner, had downed a remarkable number of brandies in a very short time. Tom was now whispering in Katrina's ear while she tickled the end of his nose with a strand of long red-gold hair.

Setting down his glass, Richter resumed his lecture. "Net profits are the difference between the total income from your sales and the cost of producing the goods sold. If your profits are too low, then either your costs are too high or your price is too low. Mathematically, there are no other possibilities."

"What's that about prices being too low?" inquired Robichaux, removing himself from Katrina's hair and rubbing his nose thoughtfully. Possibly it itched. "Are you talking about Rutledge?"

"No," said Richter impatiently, "Rutledge's profits are what's keeping National in the black. There's no room for fraud there," he added reluctantly. Rutledge was no favorite of his. "I'm talking about Blaney. He makes the same components as Rutledge, but he doesn't make the same profits. His costs are too high—*he* says. I saw him slinking out of the offices of one of our suppliers the other day."

There was a nasty silence. "You realize what you're saying," said Thatcher at length. He disliked getting information in this way, but there was no denying that Richter's theory would explain a good deal.

"Well," said Richter defiantly, "it wouldn't be the first time a division manager took a kickback from a supplier, and let the supplier set his own prices. You can't get around the fact that Blaney's costs are about twice as high as Rutledge's."

"I see. You've been doing some comparison studies, I take it," suggested Thatcher delicately.

"As much as you can in a company that doesn't let one

division have access to another division's figures. I have every right to," said Richter heatedly.

"Sure," said Robichaux amiably. "More power to you."

"And let me tell you one thing. There may be a few changes at National before all this is over." Richter drained his glass, and came to an abrupt halt.

"And what will the changes be?" asked Thatcher.

But Richter had recovered himself, and now spoke with more moderation. "I can't really tell. But I don't think you'll be going far wrong to count on the new management containing, among others of course, Allen Hammond, Jay Rutledge, and me."

Thatcher nodded thoughtfully. So that was Richter's game. It was really obvious. If Richter could talk Hammond and Rutledge into a triumvirate, then the three could be assured of survival and possibly elevation while public clamor was quieted by the removal of Blaney and Mason. But exactly how did they plan the removal? It looked very much as if railroading Harry Blaney was to be part of the strategy. Thatcher frowned thoughtfully. It would be interesting to hear the views of Hammond and Rutledge. But not half so easy. They were neither of them chatterboxes. Thatcher decided there was nothing more to be learned from Morris Richter.

"Well, that's all very interesting, Richter," he said, setting his glass down with finality, "You've been very helpful and forthcoming. I'll tell Mason what you said."

Richter paled.

"About the stolen expense accounts, of course," continued Thatcher smoothly. "And we certainly shall look up young Draper. Ready, Tom?"

"You go ahead, John," said Robichaux muzzily. "I'll stay behind if Richter doesn't mind a self-invited guest."

Richter made hostlike noises.

Katrina smiled enigmatically.

Thatcher thought of old Barnwell at Barnwell and McBridge. His duty was clear.

"Come on, Tom. We promised to have a report by tomorrow. We've still got a lot of work to do tonight."

Robichaux wavered.

Katrina laid a large and shapely hand coaxingly on his arm. Robichaux looked down at her.

"We can do it tomorrow morning, John," he said.

"Now, look, Tom—"

"Yoo hoo, Mr. Thatcher! Don't go away!"

Thatcher looked up and saw Josie Richter bearing down on him with two men. One was Georgi, reeling slightly, but cradling his balalaika tenderly in one hand and making huge detaining gestures with the other. The other man, Thatcher could feel it in his bones, was a Serb poet. To hell with Tom! He was old enough to take care of himself. You didn't see old Barnwell making a nursery maid out of himself.

"Yoo hoo!"

Thatcher fled.

# 12

# *Enter Regina*

By eleven-thirty the next morning Robichaux had still not returned the call which Thatcher made to his office promptly at nine o'clock. Annoyed, but scarcely surprised, Thatcher had spent the time very profitably with Walter Bowman, chief of the Research Staff. The research staff, of course, kept the Sloan supplied with information on its present investments. But its most important function by far was the discovery and development of new investment opportunities. Bowman's intelligence agents were deployed around the financial section, alert for the slightest hint of a new company, a new expansion, a new financing. The results of their activities were placed before the Investment Committee at one of its weekly meetings by their chief. Occasionally, however, when Walter Bowman anticipated strenuous objections to one of his pet prospects, he tried to recruit a supporting claque before the Committee meeting. And he had just passed two hours laying the groundwork for the incorporation of John Thatcher into such a claque. The conversation had opened with a discussion of the product.

"They've developed this cheap process for turning out plastic covered loose-leaf notebooks. Cuts the cost by 60 percent."

"What's so special about a plastic cover? Is it transparent?"

"No, no. It's black. Looks better, lasts longer, resists

scratching," Walter said persuasively. "Orders are pouring in."

They moved on to a spirited analysis of the probable market. Bowman dwelt fervently on the swelling school population, the increase in educational spending, the conversion of industry to the ring binder for record keeping.

Next came the need for expansion. Capacity must be quadrupled at the very least, according to Bowman.

"The demand is going to be there. They've got to be able to meet it."

"Well, it sounds pretty interesting, Walter. I'd like to see your report."

Bowman laid the folder on the table. "It makes good reading, John. The projected financials and cash flow are in the back." He rose to leave, satisfied with his interview. This was as much as he had hoped for. It was axiomatic that Thatcher never made an investment decision in Bowman's presence. "Walter's enthusiasm," he had been heard to explain, "is as infectious as German measles. He missed a great career as a confidence man."

True to his word, Thatcher settled down to devote himself to the research report. He was engaged in the fine art of picking holes in the projected financials when Miss Corsa buzzed him.

"Mr. Robichaux will be on the line in a moment, Mr. Thatcher," she announced.

Obediently, Thatcher depressed the button that connected him with the outside world. He was familiar with the situation. Robichaux and Devane was notorious for refusing alien secretaries the privilege of direct communication with its senior partners. First put your principal on, then we'll put our partner on. Surely there must be exceptions, thought Thatcher. Idly he speculated on the possibilities. The President of the United States? Nikita Khrushchev? The Pope? The last appealed to him.

Clicks and buzzes heralded the approach of a partner. Contact was established. Robichaux, while more subdued than usual, was in the best of spirits.

"You know, John," he said chattily, after an exchange of preliminaries, "that Katrina is a very interesting woman."

Thatcher was curt. "No doubt. Remember to tell Barnwell all about her. He'll be interested. In case you've forgotten, we agreed to go to National today. Let's go!"

"National?" questioned Robichaux artlessly.

"National Calculating!" Sadistically, Thatcher raised his voice to a bellow worthy of Robichaux at his best. "We're going to talk to somebody called Draper and to that leftover from your misbegotten childhood, Chip Mason."

"Anything you say, John. No need to shout," said Tom plaintively. "And maybe we could stop for a bite on the way."

"Is it time for lunch?" Thatcher looked at his watch. He had not realized that it was after twelve.

"No. Breakfast," Robichaux admitted unrepentantly.

"Oh, meet me at Child's," snarled Thatcher.

Fortified by breakfast, Robichaux was prepared to turn his mind to the problems of National.

"You think this Draper really may know something the police haven't shaken out of him yet?" he asked as he stood with Thatcher in the lobby of the Southern Bourbon Building waiting for the elevator to take them to the sixteenth floor.

"Nothing that could be used in evidence," replied Thatcher. "After all, the fact that he had the office next to Fortinbras would be the sort of thing the police would be onto immediately. But I talked with Henry Addison this morning. He's the accountant we sent down here. And he's been impressed by the fact that Draper followed Fortinbras around like a shadow. Looked up to him as a great man, and drank in every word. Quite apart from his knowledge of the expense accounts, Draper may have some idea of the direction Fortinbras's suspicions were taking."

"You don't think he'd have told the police?" asked Robichaux dubiously.

"Not if he just had a hint dropped by Fortinbras. After all, he works for these people. He's not likely to rush into accusations he can't substantiate."

Robichaux refrained from answering as the elevator arrived and they were joined by a rush of National employees returning from lunch. Several of them exchanged nods and greetings with the two men. Robichaux and Thatcher were becoming familiar sights, and a number of people were under the impression that they had recently joined the payroll. Their treatment at the hands of the receptionist would have served to confirm such a belief. She contented herself with waving them on into Mary Sullivan's bailiwick.

Mary Sullivan, although severely tried by the events of the past week, was still maintaining the standards of the front office. She greeted them cordially and announced that Mr. Mason would be delighted to learn of their arrival.

But Thatcher could hear the sound of voices from behind the door to the chief executive's office. "There's no need for us to disturb Mr. Mason while he's busy. We wanted to speak with a Mr. Stanley Draper first, anyway. If you could arrange that for us," he suggested, "we'll come back here later."

A wealth of meaning entered Mary Sullivan's voice. "But Mr. Mason would be delighted to see you now. It wouldn't be an interruption at all."

Thatcher had no problem interpreting this hint. More trouble. Scarcely surprising. He cocked his head in an attempt to understand the voices. There seemed to be a good many.

"Doesn't sound very friendly," remarked Robichaux cheerfully.

"All right," capitulated Thatcher.

Miss Sullivan immediately did things with her intercom and received a terse instruction from her employer.

"Will you go right in, Mr. Thatcher?" she invited with a grateful smile.

Robichaux and Thatcher entered upon a crowded scene, and their appearance caused the participants to freeze in a tableau suggesting the curtain scene of Act Two. The center of the stage was held by a medium-sized elderly woman dressed in a mink coat which the knowledgeable Robichaux immediately eyed with respect. She was standing bolt up-right with her right forefinger dramatically extended toward a red-faced Mason who was mopping his brow with a large initialed handkerchief. Grouped around these two protagonists were all the leading lights of National's management.

"Come in, come in," trumpeted Mason in a desperate sort of welcome. "I don't believe you've met Mrs. Plout."

Regina Plout brushed aside introductions. "I am secretary-treasurer of the National Calculating Stockholders Protest Committee. We are going to carry on Clarence Fortinbras's work, and you can't stop us."

"Now, Mrs. Plout—"

"Don't think just because you've managed to murder Clarence, you can stop us from continuing our audit."

A subdued hubbub rose at this accusation. Allen Hammond said they should all calm down and talk things over quietly; his remarks were drowned out by Blaney's roar of protest and Rutledge's recommendation that Mrs. Plout moderate her language. Richter made reference to the law of slander, and Mrs. Cobb to the manners of a juvenile delinquent. Regina Plout happily settled down to take on all comers. Everybody started shouting.

In the midst of these proceedings a familiar face appeared at Thatcher's side.

"Good Heavens, Lee, what are you doing here?"

"Hello, Thatcher." Edward Lee quietly shook hands. "I, too, am on the stockholders' committee. I thought Mrs. Plout should have a witness for her meeting with Mason." He nodded over to the corner where Regina Plout was now energetically prodding her finger into Mason's chest.

"It doesn't seem to be a particularly fruitful meeting," said Thatcher cautiously.

Lee shrugged fastidiously. "What can you expect when vulgarity and stupidity meet head on." He brooded for a moment. "Mason is a fool!"

"Anything special he's done?" inquired Thatcher, showing no inclination to dispute Lee's reading of Mason.

"Regina has written twice for an appointment since Clarence's death. Both times she's received a reply from him saying he was too busy at the moment, but he looked forward to seeing her in the future. You can imagine her reaction to that."

"Yes," agreed Thatcher, "I can." Would nothing teach Mason? Apparently not.

Suddenly their withdrawn little group became the storm center of a new aspect of the controversy.

"Robichaux!" proclaimed Mrs. Plout in tones of scornful loathing. "We know all about him."

"Eh? What's that?" said Tom, startled into an unwise search for enlightenment. He drew the full fury of Mrs. Plout's attention.

"You're Mason's tame underwriter. An independent audit! Not very likely."

"Now see here," protested Robichaux indignantly. He received assistance from an unexpected quarter. Jay Rutledge's deep voice boomed across the room.

"Mrs. Plout, there is no question as to the independence of Robichaux and Devane. Furthermore, the New York City Police Department is participating in this audit. Are you suggesting that—"

The enormity of Regina Plout's suggestion was not elaborated. Mary Sullivan, with her usual instinct for diverting whatever furies threatened her superior, had opened the door and was quietly waiting for an opportunity to speak.

"Mr. Thatcher," she said when she had succeeded in capturing the attention of the gathering. "I've located Mr. Draper. He's in conference with the assistant controller, but he can postpone that if you wish to see him now."

"What's this?" Mason looked at her ungratefully. He addressed himself to Thatcher and Robichaux. "You can't leave now. Anyway, I want to see you after this is over. That is, after Mrs. Plout has finished." He eyed Mrs. Plout resentfully, but not unhopefully. She might take the hint.

She did not. But Thatcher did.

"Yes, we'll stay," replied Thatcher with the calm air of command that comes naturally to the unthreatened by-stander. He might yet have a chance for a quiet word with

Edward Lee, who was known to him from a course of amiable dealings with the financial needs of the Chinese Merchants Association. Lee was a sensible man of wide experience. Fortinbras might well have confided to him suspicions which would have been shrouded in silence before the hysterical Plout and the youthful Draper.

"Anybody can stay," invited Regina Plout nastily, "but it isn't going to stop me getting my rights. We have a court order to examine, and we intend to examine."

"I think perhaps you're stating our position too narrowly," Lee intervened. He had hoped to remain silent, but common decency compelled him to exercise whatever braking power he could on Mrs. Plout's redoubtable attacking potential. "We intend to see that an independent audit is pursued. If we are assured that an independent audit is being conducted by Robichaux and Devane and the Sloan Guaranty and, for that matter—" he inclined his head graciously toward Rutledge—"by the New York City Police Department, we will be quite content." He concluded this masterful paraphrase of a position diametrically opposed to that enunciated by Regina Plout with a quelling stare in her direction.

She was noticeably unmoved by this sudden display of Oriental ferocity. Neither the institution of Robichaux and Devane nor that of the New York City Police had succeeded in impressing her with its probity. But Lee's statement had still achieved its purpose.

"The Sloan Guaranty—you mean the bank?" she demanded.

Upon being assured that this was the institution in question, she was unaccountably mollified.

"They did very well with the trust Samuel left," she recalled approvingly. Then her face darkened. "I'll bet there isn't much funny business here they won't bring to light."

Blaney was imprudent enough to protest.

"Well," she retorted with offensive reasonableness. "Why did you kill Clarence if there isn't any funny business?"

"I did not kill Clarence!" howled Blaney, driven into unintentional intimacy with the deceased.

"I meant all of you." Mrs. Plout encompassed the entire gathering with a comprehensive sweep of the arm.

"Excuse me," barked Mary Sullivan briskly from the doorway. "It's your secretary, Mr. Blaney. You have a call from a Mr. Jarvey."

"Have it transferred in here, Mary," directed Mason from behind the desk, to which position he had retreated from Mrs. Plout's prodding forefinger.

"No!" shouted Blaney as Miss Sullivan retired from the room. She looked at him in astonishment. Her expression made it plain that she was not accustomed to raised voices no matter how strained the emotions of her superiors. Blaney composed himself. "I'm sorry. But would you ask her to tell Mr. Jarvey I'm in conference, and I'll call back?"

Mrs. Plout cackled triumphantly. "Ah-ha! Don't dare talk in front of us, that's what's wrong with you. And I don't blame you. Who knows what would come out?" she concluded darkly.

"Why, you interfering—" Blaney bit down sharply on the expression which sprang to his unguarded lips.

"Now, I know which one you are. You're one of the two who has plants in New Jersey. And you," she said rounding on Rutledge, "are the other one! Clarence Fortinbras told us all about it. You're both at the bottom of everything."

"No, no. Not that one," moaned Lee in an agony of mortification. Sheer bad breeding he had braced himself to endure, but blatant stupidity was too much. "He's the one who makes profits."

"I don't care. You can't tell me that they can have two plants turning out the same thing, and make money in one and lose it in the other without something being fishy. Anyway I don't like his shifty eyes."

"Well," said Rutledge with imperturbable good manners, "then I'll take my shifty eyes back to work, and make some use of my time. That is, if you have no objection, ma'am." The manners might be imperturbable, but not the man. Nothing finds a courtly Southerner so defenseless as a shrew. There was a perceptible rasp in the steady low drawl.

"There now," said Regina, viewing his retreat with satisfaction, "Not a word to say for himself."

"On the contrary," said Allen Hammond in tones of cold rebuke, "he doesn't have to say anything for himself. Nor, I might add, do the rest of us. You have been assured of the continuation of the audit commenced by Mr. Fortinbras. In place of these vague insinuations, are there any other demands which you or Mr. Lee care to make on us?"

"Why is he trying to drag me into this?" muttered Edward Lee resentfully.

Absently Thatcher made soothing noises. Hammond's manner was not calculated to inspire affection. Even Mason was bending a suspicious glance toward his nephew. This was very much the tone of the "head of the firm." Some slight concession to his uncle's presence would not only have been tactful, it would have been in character. It needed only the thoughtful look on Richter's face to confirm Thatcher's feeling that Hammond had just crossed a Rubicon of some sort. Two-thirds of the triumvirate had lined up. One more and the coalition was made.

Mrs. Plout also was not disposed to admire the new look at National.

"What do we demand? We demand that the killer of Clarence Fortinbras be handed over to the police. We demand that the rest of you get out—incompetents at best, that's what Clarence said," she screeched. "We demand to know who's been lining his pockets."

Into the hush of anticipation that followed this alarming catalog of demands came a breath of fresh air. The door had opened unnoticed during Mrs. Plout's tirade. Now Barney Young stood on the threshold, surveying the group with an air of confident delight. He advanced to the center of the room to share the stage with Regina. "Look, folks," he caroled, "I wanted you to be first to see. I've got some pictures of the baby." Heedless of the hiss of indrawn breaths, he shoved some snapshots into Mrs. Plout's outflung hand. "Polaroid shots," he confided. "Took them myself."

From Richter's corner came the sound of an imperfectly controlled and perfectly audible high, male giggle.

Mason turned purple.

Blaney turned white.

Richter exploded into helpless laughter, and Allen Hammond walked over to a speechless John Thatcher and began to explain the unhappy circumstances into which Barney Young seemed destined to intrude paternal pride.

# 13

## *Exit Stanley*

The front office of National Calculating might dissipate its energies coping with belligerent stockholders, wilting executives and ruffled employees (Barney Young had been hurt, very hurt), but down on the fifteenth floor when five o'clock came, three men were able to pack up for the night in conscious rectitude of having accomplished a solid day's work. They entered final totals, ripped tapes out of adding machines and attached them to relevant schedules, and returned files to cabinets which boasted padlocked iron bars as well as combination locks. Someone might still attempt to disrupt the Great Audit by stealing papers, but this time he would have to do it with a blowtorch.

"I've got the list of things you want tomorrow morning," said Stanley Draper as his two companions surveyed the bare, orderly room with satisfaction.

"Good." Henry Addison grunted as the zipper on his briefcase balked at a corner.

"Mr. Fortinbras used soap on his. He said it stopped the sticking for a couple of weeks." Stanley hovered tentatively in the doorway.

Snapping the catches on his attaché case, Fred Cohen agreed. "A lot of people say it helps."

Still Stanley did not leave. No one had any doubt as to what was bothering him. Everybody at National Calculating knew that the accountants had found something, that memoranda had gone forth, that Mr. Mason had been in communication with Messrs. Thatcher and Robichaux, that these two gentlemen had descended in person. There were rumors of nighttime meetings with Dr. Richter and sensational exposés in the offing. And Stanley had been told nothing.

He felt it keenly.

The two older men had therefore been exceedingly kind all day. Stanley's lightest remark had been received with deep attention. Eager questions followed every reminiscence about Fortinbras. No one interrupted. Orders took the form of mild requests and timid attempts by Stanley to fish for information had been smoothly evaded instead of sternly squelched.

Now Fred Cohen paid the day's final tribute to Stanley's sensitivities.

"If you wait a minute, Stanley, we can all go down to the street together."

The crowd in the hallway milling around the bank of elevators effectively put an end to any further displays of curiosity, and inside the elevator put an end to any conversation whatsoever. Everyone was fully occupied clutching hats, briefcases, umbrellas, raincoats, rubbers, and all the other paraphernalia of working New York on a rainy autumn evening.

Once emerged into the lobby, the homeward-bound group could see that the afternoon's steady downpour had been augmented by winds of hurricane proportions. The great double-storied glass frontage of the Southern Bourbon Building mirrored the tidal wave of humanity streaming toward subways and bus stops. Men with upturned collars were hunched against the wind, gripping their hatbrims with ferocious determination. Women fought with both hands against the pull of their umbrellas. Sheets of spray were sent up from the street with every passing vehicle, and from nowhere sodden folds of newspaper swirled aloft until they smacked down into the gutters.

Henry Addison took one look, and grounded his belongings in order to strap himself together against the onslaught of the elements. His two companions waited for him, patiently stepping aside to allow the passage of a contingent from the sixteenth floor.

Jay Rutledge, looking very tired, settled his hat more firmly, nodded good night, and passed through the revolving doors. Morris Richter and Allen Hammond had a final exchange at the end of which Hammond snapped something inaudible and shouldered his way to the exit. Richter's affronted gaze followed his retreat for a moment, then the sight of Chip Mason being debouched in lordly isolation spurred the scientist into hasty movement. The president of National Calculating disentangled himself from a gaggle of typists, and punctiliously paused to acknowledge the presence of alien forces on his territory. Stanley was scrupulously included in his wishes that the accountants should enjoy a well-earned evening of rest.

"Very polite," murmured Cohen suspiciously as Addison indicated that he was ready for the plunge outdoors.

Stanley protested that Mr. Mason was always polite.

"Fortinbras." Cohen reminded him.

Well, yes, Stanley had to admit that occasionally Mr. Mason had been a little short with Mr. Fortinbras.

"It's because we're institutional," explained Addison. "That makes us acceptable."

Cohen nodded. Both men were used to situations in which their persons represented not Henry Addison, aged forty-two, and Fred Cohen, aged fifty-four, but the Sloan Guaranty Trust and the New York City Police Department. Under these circumstances they received a good deal of unlooked-for civility.

But Stanley, who alas represented nothing, thought maybe Mr. Mason had been setting one of those good examples for which he was justly famous. Perhaps they hadn't noticed Mr. Blaney barging out without a word to anyone?

As they turned east to walk to Lexington Avenue the wind, howling dementedly over their heads in the narrow canyon, lost some of the force it displayed on its southward sweep down the avenues, and the two older men had the opportunity for a polite pretense of interest in Stanley's troubles commuting to Yonkers. He was bound for a bus to take him to Grand Central where the real effort of the evening would begin. Thankfully they announced that the subway was their destination and the only conveyance involved in their trip home. For some reason Stanley seemed to associate their freedom from rail transport with their status in the accounting profession.

It was with a good deal of relief that his two companions deposited Stanley at his bus stop and themselves turned north for a two-block walk to the subway station.

"There's no denying that he's a nice boy," said Cohen, sadly examining his sodden trouser cuffs as they waited for the light to change. "But he can be tiring."

Addison peered into the darkening gloom lit by the reflection of headlights from the wetly gleaming asphalt. "Here we go," he announced as the last crosstown racer sped through. "Yes, he's difficult. Partly it's his isolation, I expect. If he had a coffee klatch to gossip with, he wouldn't bother us so . . ."

A scream of tires braked into a sharp skid interrupted him. From the bus crowd half a block back came a shrill woman's scream. Suddenly the normal cacophony of five-thirty noises was pierced and overridden by the blasting of police whistles. Hundreds of excited human voices swelled into incoherent commentary. Traffic came to a grinding halt, and the center of disturbance swelled as if by magic with the instantaneous accretion of scurrying spectators.

The two men who had instinctively swung around suddenly broke into a run.

"Pardon me, madam . . ."

"If you'll just let me through . . ."

"Sorry . . ."

Their movements became brusker and their apologies terser as they elbowed their way to the front lines. Here a complicated knot of people screened from their sight the figure on the ground.

A small man, heedless of the rain streaming down his bare head, had both hands pressed to his face.

"My God, I was swinging around the bus. I didn't see him. I braked as soon as I could."

"That's right." The bus driver had emerged from his vehicle and now entered the conversation. "I saw the whole thing. It was a green light, and he wasn't speeding. Suddenly this guy came shooting out of the mob in front of the bus and right into the road."

The driver moaned gently. "Is he dead? How bad is he hurt? Christ, I'll never drive a car again."

The busman placed a sustaining hand on his shoulder. "Look, it wasn't your fault. You can't help it if some fool goes charging out on a green light . . ."

"I'll want statements from both of you." The policeman who had been kneeling by the still figure and obscuring it from view rose to his feet. "He's not dead, but he doesn't look good to me. The ambulance'll be here in a minute. So will the traffic detail. Jesus, it would happen in rush hour." He looked up the length of Lexington Avenue which was now black with a solid mass of backed-up traffic stretching as far as could be seen. From several blocks away came the insistent blaring of horns from motorists unaware of the reason for the tie-up.

Henry Addison gave a series of hopping little jumps to see over the shoulder of the tall sailor standing directly in his path. The victim was a thin man in a raincoat. But he couldn't be sure . . . everybody was wearing a raincoat today. Fred Cohen, the taller by several inches, put his doubts to rest.

"It's Stanley," he said grimly.

They looked at each other in silence. Dimly they heard the participants around the prone figure.

"Look," the policeman was saying in kindlier tones as a blinking red light down the middle of the street indicated the arrival of reinforcements, "traffic accidents just happen. You don't want to go all to pieces if it wasn't your fault. I've got three witnesses that say you couldn't have done a thing to prevent it. One minute you had a clear road and the next minute he was right smack in front of you."

"If you ask me, he'd been drinking," said a stout, befurred woman. "He just staggered out. And, Officer, I think this man needs treatment for shock. You don't have heart trouble or anything?" she asked anxiously.

"No, no, I'll be all right. When is that ambulance coming?"

Henry Addison shook the drops from his hat. "I suppose it could have been an accident," he said doubtfully. "They happen all the time."

"Sure." Cohen agreed in carefully neutral tones. "And this is just the kind of night when they happen. No visibility, bad surface for braking, millions of people spilling off the sidewalks."

"Well," said Addison heavily, "the least we can do is identify him, and find out what hospital they take him to."

There was a moment of silence in which a distant siren began to make itself heard. Cohen chose his words with care. "Yes, it certainly wouldn't hurt to do that. And I suppose, just for the record of course, the connection ought to be made."

Addison nodded. Cohen obviously shared his views on the credibility of the accident. Unbidden, the vision of the lobby of the Southern Bourbon Building rose before his mind. Rutledge, Hammond, Richter, Mason and—if Stanley Draper had been right—Blaney as well. All of them at the critical time no more than two crosstown blocks from the scene. Any one of them could have been right behind their little threesome. This was just the kind of night for that to happen as well as bona fide traffic mishaps. Who would notice who stalked cautiously behind in this kind of weather? All three of them had been hunched forward, with hats pulled low, and the wind whistling in their ears. Every pedestrian was a little island unto himself with all the senses that normally connected him with the outside world muffled and distorted by the assault on sight and sound.

An involuntary shiver ran down Addison's back. It was not a pleasant thought, this picture of them plodding along dutifully listening to a recital of ordinary commuter woes while behind them prowled an anonymous figure, lost in the city's crowd, patiently prepared to follow them for blocks in the certainty that sooner or later, what had actually happened would occur. That Stanley would be cut out from the fold, just like a straggling sheep, and left as a target for attack.

"What's that?" Addison had missed what Cohen had been saying.

"I said I think we'd better wait until the ambulance has gone and he's writing up names and addresses in his notebook."

"Yes, yes, of course . . . you know, if what we're thinking is true, Stanley must have known something."

Cohen, with native caution, was inclined to temporize. "We're not thinking anything. We just want the relevant facts in the record."

"All right, all right," said Addison impatiently, feeling they had already made enough concessions to the civil servant's reluctance to commit himself. "But I could have sworn there wasn't anything. Stanley practically turned himself inside out cooperating."

"It wouldn't have to be much. And he wouldn't have to realize it was important. To him it could be something too insignificant to repeat. But to the man who strangled Fortinbras, it could mean the electric chair."

Yes, of course, they were dealing with a man who had already killed once. If Fortinbras had been right, and neither Cohen nor Addison was inclined to dispute this supposition for a second, then they were faced with a man vulnerable on two fronts. Fraud and murder—both open to detection. No, by now he was not likely to be a man prepared to allow the continued existence of any threat to his safety, no matter how small, no matter how improbable the threat.

The ambulance men had worked swiftly. As they lifted the stretcher through the back doors, the crowd began to melt away, and Addison could hear the intern say a few words to the policeman.

"Oh, he's got a chance. But not a very good one. They'll operate as soon as he gets to the hospital. We've radioed them. But you'd better get in touch with his relatives right away. And find out if he's Catholic."

The ambulance driver beckoned. The intern swung himself inside, and they started to drive away. They were using the siren.

Cohen was already edging his way forward. A touch on the arm, a flourish of the identification card in his wallet, and the traffic officer was bending over to listen to him.

"Yes, the murder case at the Southern Bourbon Building. Have a copy of your report sent to Lieutenant Francis Cortell, Homicide. That's right. He'll want it as soon as possible."

Cohen turned back to Addison. "That's about it for now. At least Cortell will know about it. He won't bother you tonight. But better be prepared to spend an hour or so with him tomorrow. He'll want to hear your story." Cohen paused unhappily and decided he was being too alarmist. "Just for the record, you know."

Addison nodded impassively. "Certainly. Any time Lieutenant Cortell wants me. I'll be at the Sloan or at National Calculating."

"That's fine."

"Will you have any news about Stanley? I'd like to find out."

"Call the hospital tomorrow morning. They've taken him to Bellevue."

From his experience with hospitals, Addison took this to mean that the New York Police might regard information about Stanley Draper's condition as classified. And if a murderer was going to be taking an interest, it was just as well.

Respecting Cohen's retreat behind the wall of official reserve, Addison decided to forgo any further questions or speculations. The spot where they stood was rapidly returning to normal. The bus was loading its passengers. The traffic detail started to remove the barriers diverting cars into crosstown streets and over to Park Avenue. The beating rain had already erased from the street the pathetically insignificant stains marking the place where Stanley had fallen.

It was time to go home.

Addison indicated the sidewalk with a questioning glance,

but Cohen, frowning abstractedly at the small crowd of die-hards under a shop window awning, shook his head.

"No, if you don't mind, I think I'll give the subway a miss. A taxi will be quicker."

He gestured to a cabbie whose indignant fare had abandoned him during the tie-up.

Addison stepped back but he could still overhear the instructions to the cabbie.

"Police Headquarters. Centre Street."

So much for Cohen's elaborate detachment. He had meant to speed to Lieutenant Cortell's side all the time. As accountants they might stand on a peerlike basis, shoulder to shoulder. But when a suspicion of foul play had arisen, Cohen felt the need to shed his civilian associates and retire into the bosom of his colleagues. Well, that was understandable, thought Addison unresentfully as a splash from the curb made him dodge rapidly into a woman huddled under her umbrella.

Mechanically he apologized and continued his progress. Fifty yards up the street he paused. He had not seen the woman clearly. She had not acknowledged his courtesy, but had merely drawn back protectively under her shelter. Why then was he haunted by an elusive familiarity? She had been just like any other woman on this night of faceless, depersonalized human beings. A woman in a plastic raincoat and hood, with a purse. No, not a purse. A briefcase. And the woman was Dr. Cobb of National Calculating.

So . . .

Perhaps he had done Cohen an injustice. Perhaps the decision to go to Centre Street had been taken on the spur of the moment, as Cohen examined the crowd under the awning and recognized a figure he knew. A figure which, as Addison turned to survey the path by which he had come, had now disappeared. It was odd, very odd. And he had drawn for himself such a convincing portrait of their unknown pursuer. Could he have been wrong in the only characteristic he had assigned to that formless adversary?

It was disturbing and somehow ominous. He found himself quickening his steps toward the bustling subway station. Not the least disturbing element was the thought of his coming interview with John Putnam Thatcher. His audit had assumed a dimension unlikely to recommend itself to the senior vice president of the Sloan.

# 14

## Of Trumpets and Ordnance

But Henry Addison did not plunge into the subway. After a brief debate with himself, he went instead to a nearby public telephone and dialed the Sloan. He was lucky enough to catch John Thatcher just as he returned to his office to pick up some papers. Addison was a perfectly self-confident man, but he did not relish the prospect of disturbing Thatcher in the privacy of his home. Particularly with this kind of news.

Thatcher listened to his bald account of the accident to Stanley Draper, then fell into a silence so extended that Addison, uncomfortably damp in the telephone box, wondered if they had been disconnected.

"What? Oh, sorry, Addison. No, I'm here. Well, there's nothing we can do tonight. Will you stop at the bank tomorrow morning to give me a fuller rundown? Before you go over to National? I'll be here early."

He was. And looking very somber as he listened to Henry Addison's extended description of the accident.

"Is the boy still alive this morning?" he asked.

"Just barely," Addison replied. "Cohen called me before I left the house. Stanley's in pretty bad shape."

Thatcher frowned. "Do you know if the police have been able to question him?"

Stanley Draper had been unconscious since the accident. His young and frightened wife was at his bedside, with his distraught parents. But Stanley could speak to none of them. It was by no means certain that Stanley would ever speak again.

"Damn them," said Thatcher obscurely. "Did you say that the police have posted a guard?"

Addison nodded.

"That means they think it was a murder attempt," Thatcher said more to himself than to Addison. He looked up. "And you do too."

Addison preferred statements of fact to statements of opinion. He replied that the police were making a careful check of the evening rush-hour traffic out of National Calculating.

Thatcher heard him out, then said, "Well, for God's sake, be careful!" He sounded irascible.

Addison smiled slightly. "We're getting a police guard too," he said. "Working with Cohen is an education in many ways."

After he left, Thatcher twirled his chair around to stare absently out of his window.

Five minutes later, Miss Corsa appeared, dictation book in hand, interrupting a train of thought that had given him no pleasure at all.

He turned to look soberly at her.

"Somebody has tried to kill young Stanley Draper," he said.

Miss Corsa, an extremely unemotional young woman, registered nothing more than polite interest.

"Draper," Thatcher continued emphatically, "Draper was the accountant at National Calculating that I wanted to talk to today. No, let me correct that. I did not want to talk to him, but I felt that I should discuss these missing expense accounts with him. And now he has been run over. It could have been a traffic accident, Miss Corsa, but you and I know better, don't we? We know that Clarence Fortinbras was strangled with an electric cord on the premises of that miserable outfit, and when one of his associates is run down, we know what that means, don't we?" He glowered at her.

"I don't," she replied composedly. Miss Corsa had long

since abandoned any attempt to enter into the spirit of the thing with Mr. Thatcher.

"It means," he snapped, "that I have had more than enough of National Calculating. Let the police take over! We've tried to save that idiot Mason, and that idiot Claster, as well—by the way, send a memo to the Investment Division congratulating him on National's growth potential—but two murders can't be hushed up—" He broke off and considered his own words. If Stanley Draper did not survive, a murderer would have struck twice at National Calculating. Miss Corsa, unmoved, waited. "Two murders and it becomes academic to try saving the market in National Calculating. Do I make myself clear?"

"I don't . . ."

"Good! Now, Miss Corsa, this means that as of this moment, I am washing my hands—and figuratively, I am washing the Sloan's hands—of the whole imbroglio. Do you understand?"

"Certainly . . ."

"Your role in this, Miss Corsa, is to aid and abet me. No telephone calls from anyone even remotely connected with the whole affair. That means Mr. Mason. That means Mr. Addison. That means Mr. Claster. That means Mr. Robichaux. . . ."

Miss Corsa stood up. "Certainly, Mr. Thatcher," she said, a shade of reproof in her voice. "Do you want to dictate now?"

"Not at the moment," he said ferociously.

She left him to stew in the juice of his own rancor.

Despite his pronouncements, John Thatcher devoted the next half hour to a hardheaded analysis of possible means of salvaging something from the catastrophe at National Calculating. He finally concluded that although he would be asked to do more, there was nothing more he could profitably do.

Left in a very bad mood, he decided to utilize his splenetic energy. "Miss Corsa," he barked over the intercom, "send Charlie Trinkam in here."

And to that worldling's pained surprise, the head of the Trust Department gave him a very hard hour over some recent developments in the Sloan's utilities holdings.

In fact, Thatcher recorded an impressive volume of achievement during the day, working at a steady pace that not only cleared the desk of the accumulation that had mounted during his forays on behalf of National Calculating, but reduced several subordinates to their knees.

"If he's in his office," Everett Gabler said fussily, "I think I'll drop in and talk to him about Inimicon. I don't like . . ."

"Just to show you that I'm a good sort," Charlie Trinkam said as he sucked a healing lungful of smoke, "I'll give you a word of advice: don't."

At three o'clock, Miss Corsa, looking harried, appeared in the office.

"It's Mr. Robichaux," she explained. "He's insisting . . ."

Beneath Thatcher's steely regard, her voice faltered.

"No, Miss Corsa," he said gently.

Thatcher worked uninterruptedly until five-thirty, then decided to abandon the burdens of high place for a restful evening at home, when Miss Corsa struck back.

"You won't forget the Animal Rescue League?" she said, preparing to leave despite unfinished letters on her desk, a sure sign of her disapproval.

He scowled at her.

"Mrs. Carlson called this afternoon to tell me to be sure to remind you to come to the dinner and ball for the Animal Rescue League," Miss Corsa said. Then, playing her trump card, "It's at the Biltmore, Mrs. Carlson said. White tie. Good night, Mr. Thatcher."

Poleaxed, John Thatcher sank back in his chair as Vengeance put on her coat and left the office. He examined the fearful implications of Miss Corsa's message; dimly, he recalled a promise extracted by his daughter Laura to support this deserving cause. Ominous details began to drift to the surface of his memory.

"It isn't the money," Laura had said, pocketing his substantial check. "But I want you to promise to come to the ball. We want to have a big turnout."

"I'll come," he had recklessly promised.

He stretched a hand to the phone, then let it fall. There was nothing to be gained from calling Laura and expecting to be excused; she had inherited her mother's high sense of service, and some of her ability to impress it on those less high-minded than herself.

Dinner and Grand Ball for the Animal Rescue League it must be.

Thus, at ten-thirty that evening, John Putnam Thatcher smiled dutifully at his daughter and, obeying the message in her eyes, led Mrs. August Bertolling through a waltz.

"Why don't you go home?" that redoubtable old lady said as they twirled competently around the floor. "You look tired, John."

"I'm enjoying this dance enormously . . ."

"Don't talk nonsense," she said imperiously. "You never did like dancing, I recall. Not even when you were young and lively, and I was pretty. Why should you like it now?"

"I admit that tennis is my normal exercise, Sarah, but Laura said . . ."

"You men! Letting that chit of a girl run your life. Be a man. Go home and go to bed!"

Thatcher took her at her word. After restoring the dowager to her party, he assured himself that Laura was involved on the other side of the floor, then took his farewell of the other hostesses, exchanged a long-suffering look with Dr. Ben Carlson, who lounged unhappily in a gilt chair unequal to his height, and left the Grand Ballroom.

He did not make the novice's mistake of slinking out furtively. On the contrary, he held his head at a confident angle, and advanced to the hallway, every inch the important man of affairs. Waiters scurrying about could see at a glance that John Putnam Thatcher was a somebody.

He nearly made it.

"Daddy!"

Laura came flowing out after him, very grand in a gauzy green ball gown. "You're not going?"

"Well, Laura, I thought I would run along . . ."

She frowned at him, and prepared to remonstrate, when,

as her mother had before her, she smiled instead, a twinkle in her eyes. Roguishly, she cocked her head. "All right," she said, suddenly, "you can go. And . . . thank you for coming! I was very proud of you. You were the best-looking man in the room!" She stood on tiptoe to plant a kiss on his chin, then swept away to the ballroom.

John Thatcher was still smiling as he stepped out of the elevator into the lobby. Man is born to be putty in the hands of woman, and he had been putty in some very pretty hands. Not all of them daughters, either.

He started to put on his coat, when he found himself swept by a party of college students into the path of two men who were just entering the foyer.

"Sorry . . . why John Thatcher!"

Jay Rutledge, looking weary around the eyes, greeted him. He glanced at Thatcher's sartorial grandeur, and to Thatcher's admiration said nothing. Not the least of the evils of formal attire is the whimsy it elicits. Rutledge, however, showed no desire for banter. "Have you met General Cartwright? General, this is Mr. Thatcher, vice president of the Sloan Guaranty Trust . . ."

Thatcher found himself shaking hands with Miss Corsa's handsome young man. On close inspection, he did not have the preternatural youthfulness of his photographs. His face was decently lined, and he looked like a suitably mature forty-seven-year-old. It was the accident of bone structure, together with the shock of corn yellow hair, that made General Cartwright a photographer's delight. Noting his quiet manner and contained look, Thatcher reflected that a kinder fate would have made him fat and bald.

"Why don't you join us for a drink?" Rutledge continued.

Thatcher was about to demur when he was struck by the warmth of the invitation. And General Cartwright was regarding him almost hopefully. He knew full well the bone-deep fatigue that prolonged negotiations can induce in the participants. Even with the best intentions in the world, they become surfeited with each other. The benevolence induced by Laura's kiss moved him.

"Delighted," he said untruthfully, moving with them in the general direction of the men's bar.

"We finished up at about nine o'clock, and decided to come down for a drink," Rutledge explained in a random fashion as the waiter took their order.

There followed an awkward pause. Rutledge, who seemed to have lost weight almost steadily since Thatcher had first seen him, stared with somnolent intensity at his drink when it arrived, while Cartwright evinced certain signs of embarrassment. The trouble, Thatcher realized, was that everybody was reluctant to raise the one topic common to all of them; National Calculating. He steeled himself to take the plunge, when the General forestalled him.

"I spent last night with Mrs. Cobb and her husband," he told Rutledge and Thatcher. "Now there is a lady who knows about computers." This was clearly a compliment to National Calculating, and Rutledge roused himself to reply.

"Margaret Cobb is probably the most competent scientist we've ever had at National," he agreed. "She's been with us for years . . ."

"I was wondering about that," Thatcher broke in, his interview with Morris Richter fresh in his mind. "Why hasn't she ever been appointed Director of Research and Development. Mind you, I know nothing about these things. Your Dr. Richter . . ."

General Cartwright looked pained by this calculated indiscretion, but Rutledge was unruffled.

"He's not my Dr. Richter," he replied with a smile. "Young Richter's too bright for the likes of me." He sounded mildly amused. "I think Chip Mason had the idea that Research and Development might come up with the sort of thing they came up with at Polaroid. You know, basic research that could really pay off. Naturally that means a young genius, and Mrs. Cobb didn't fit . . ."

"She's certainly one smart woman," the General insisted with quiet loyalty.

"Oh, no one doubts it. And among the three of us, she's more than kept that division together through a lot of bright young men. I suspect that she'll be there after Dr. Richter is gone." He paused for a moment, and Thatcher wondered if he were going to comment on Richter's plans for a Hammond-Rutledge-Richter alliance. If he had anything to say along those lines, he thought better of it. "You know how it is. She lacks glamour . . ."

Surprisingly this appealed to the General. "It's just like the service," he said with some satisfaction. "Some years, you can't get the time of day unless you're a big guided-missile man. It all depends on what's in style." Amused by this view of the military, Thatcher looked at him, an eyebrow raised. "Now me," Cartwright continued seriously, "I'm in style some years, then I'm out of style some years. I'm conventional ground weapons, you know, and I really hit my peak during Korea. That's when I got my third star."

Thatcher felt his spirits rising, whether with the brandy or the General he could not tell.

"I suppose it's the same all over," Rutledge drawled. "Whether it's industry or the army. You know, in places where we're having all of these scientific discoveries, we have a terrible time convincing people that old fogies like Margaret Cobb and me know anything at all." He spoke with the comfortable assurance of the man who had developed the TCR, tolerant of the brash young Richters of the world.

"What I liked about Mrs. Cobb," Cartwright continued, "is that she's easy to be with. Doesn't try to make you feel how smart she is, if you know what I mean. Of course, she was feeling a little low."

"Low?" Thatcher was startled into asking. A Mrs. Cobb who was anything but calmly efficient and detached required some readjustment in his thinking.

"I think," Cartwright said with some delicacy, "I think she and her husband were a little upset about the troubles they're having down at National."

Before Thatcher could press him, Rutledge interrupted with a wry smile. "General, you've been around National so much in the last few weeks that I think that it's a lucky thing you can tell the police you spent last evening with the

Cobbs. I was on my way home, worse luck." He looked up at Thatcher. "I take it that you must have heard about the latest bad news?"

"Stanley Draper?"

Rutledge nodded. "They're not at all sure they can save him," he said. "My secretary called at five o'clock."

Gloom redescended until the General, whose instincts were kindly, broke the silence.

"I think the best thing," he said, gesturing for a second round of drinks, "I think the best thing would be to have that lively woman turn out to be the person who killed Fortinbras. And pushed young Draper—if he was pushed."

Rutledge and Thatcher exchanged puzzled looks.

"Lively woman? Do you mean Miss Sullivan?"

"No, no . . ."

"What lively woman?"

"That woman who was kicking up such a storm yesterday afternoon . . ."

"Good Lord, General," Thatcher exclaimed as light dawned. "Did you encounter Mrs. Plout?"

"I did," he replied simply. A wintry look of disapproval crossed his face, and a new note entered his voice. The note, Thatcher realized, of a man who had commanded. "I won't say anything against a lady, but that woman doesn't know how to behave. I told her so."

"You told her so?"

"With courtesy, I hope. But it just got me pretty angry. She was shouting at me. And she said some pretty mean things to Harry Blaney . . ."

Thatcher allowed his imagination to toy with an encounter between the General and Mrs. Plout. "I wish Tom Robichaux had been there to see it," he remarked.

"Did she turn on Blaney again?" Rutledge asked.

"She did indeed. You missed the full scene."

"I'm like the General," Rutledge said with a grin that transformed his rather severe face. "When I saw Mrs. Plout blowing up a storm, I sort of sidled away."

"Wise man."

Mrs. Plout had saddened the General, whom life had hith-

erto insulated from the species. "I like a little spirit," he
said, "But the things that woman said! Why, she turned on
poor old Barney Young about his family! And he's so proud.
You know, I had lunch with him the day the baby came,
and you never saw a man feeling so good. We picked out
the cigars together. You'd think when a man has had a son
after six little girls he'd get a little appreciation. It's kind of
hard luck on him . . ."

The elemental simplicity of this view of the catastrophes
raining on National Calculating proved irresistibly appeal-
ing to Thatcher. He laughed, and after a moment Rutledge
and Cartwright joined him.

"Although I don't know why I should laugh," Rutledge
said with a rueful chuckle. "Life is pretty hard down at
National these days." He was about to continue, decided
against it, and instead took another sip of brandy.

Thatcher could find nothing in the picture of National
Calculating Corporation to cheer him, but again the United
States Army came to the rescue.

"Well, Jay, there's no denying that you've got a little trouble on your hands. And I wouldn't want to see one of my
officers behaving the way old Harry Blaney was carrying on
today. But look on the bright side. You have some good
people, you have a good product, and all of this will blow
over. You don't win all the battles, you know."

The long patience of the soldier. While it did not materi-
ally alter John Thatcher's opinion of National's outlook, he
felt, quite unreasonably, more easy in his mind about American defense policy than he had for a long time.

# 15

## Behind the Arras

Thatcher was quite honest when he told himself, Miss Corsa, and—with some detail—Tom Robichaux, that he was washing his hands of National Calculating. He resolutely beat down the flicker of sympathy roused by Jay Rutledge's worn face, bade a cordial farewell to General Cartwright with every expectation of never seeing him again (unless on the cover of *Life*) and prepared to go about his own business.

But Fate and his own besetting curiosity had something different in store for him.

He was walking back to his office after lunch the next day, hurrying a little against the first hint of winter toward the Sloan entrance on Broad Street. Thatcher, unlike some of his colleagues—Bradford Withers, for example, and Everett Gabler—was not pained by the sight of the Sloan's commercial banking facilities in the lobby. The sight of currency passing through tellers' cages was not inconsonant with his own view of the Sloan's dignity, and he cheerfully took a shortcut through the bustling bank to get to the elevators, instead of walking around the corner to the more chaste entrance of the Sloan's Executive Offices.

He was nearly at the great glass door when he came upon them: three men exuding complacent goodwill, standing in a self-congratulatory group just outside the bank, each attired in the most expensively correct business suit, and all oblivious to the lunchtime crowds eddying around them.

Public expression of ebullient spirits, however common on Madison Avenue and on Fourteenth Street, is rare on Wall Street. Thatcher well remembered old Alton Custis, whose every additional million in soybean futures brought increased melancholy to his countenance. He had been exceptional, perhaps, but generally men of the Street aim at decent sobriety, leaving jubilation to youngsters in training programs.

What halted Thatcher was the fact that one of the men was Harry Blaney. National Calculating's chief of Commercial Sales had seemed to him a badly shaken man, a man who could only imperfectly control himself in the face of the irritants and crises he was encountering.

But here he stood in front of the Sloan, full-cheeked and chuckling, the picture of undisturbed self-confidence. As Thatcher watched, he pumped the hand of one of his companions and joined the other, striding off in the general direction of Trinity Church, vigor and prosperity proclaimed by every inch of him.

Thatcher was roused by a peevish voice at his shoulder, wanting to know if he was going to build a house on the spot. He murmured apologies, and trailed Blaney's companion into the marble-glassed splendor of the Sloan's lobby.

And here he was hooked by his own curiosity as neatly as a trout. Had he nodded to Donovan the guard, strolled through the lobby to the elevators, and proceeded to the sixth floor, he could have gone about his own business with impunity. Instead he loitered in front of the check desks at the wall, and watched Blaney's friend go up to a teller, cash a check, and exchange a pleasantry—there was a burst of laughter—then turn to leave. He passed Thatcher on his way out, a sallow-faced man of about forty wearing heavy dark-rimmed glasses. He hit a brisk pace, and disappeared through the doors into the sea of humanity beating against the bank.

Thatcher watched him thoughtfully, then without pausing for reflection, went to the floor manager's office and let himself in.

"Mr. Thatcher!" Henley murmured, deference and surprise in his voice.

"Don't get up. I just want to go down to the tellers' windows."

"Good heavens! Nothing wrong, I hope . . ."

"No, I just want a little information."

Thatcher moved to the long hallway which led to the tellers' windows, nodded to the guard who looked at him with the impersonal suspicion of his kind until reassured by a nervous Henley, and was admitted to the tellers' offices.

"Will you ask the teller in Number One to step out for a moment?" he asked Miss Fellows, who looked up at him from her desk. She goggled for a moment, then ducked out to deliver the message, and Thatcher, irritably drumming his fingers on a filing cabinet, considered the perpetual apprehension under which most people condemn themselves to live. He was neither savage nor malevolent, yet his mere appearance reduced Henley to palpitations while Miss Fellows, a paragon of efficiency, was quite pale as she obeyed his request.

They probably compensated by bullying their subordinates.

Or possibly they were making plans to embezzle a million dollars. A disturbing thought.

"You wanted me, Mr. Thatcher?" he heard a youthful voice ask.

"Yes," he said to the sandy-haired young man who approached, Miss Fellows hovering behind him. "You just cashed a check for a man in a dark gray business suit and horn-rimmed glasses. About forty . . ."

"Yes," the clerk said calmly. He did not appear to be intimidated, or interested. "That's Mr. Jarvey. He has a regular commercial account . . ."

"In what name?"

"Execulit, Incorporated. They have offices across the street, 15 Broad."

Thatcher frowned, giving Miss Fellows a very nasty feeling in the pit of her stomach. Jarvey? He had heard the name before . . . of course! It was a message from a Mr.

Jarvey that had roused Regina Plout to her denunciation of
Harry Blaney! A message from Mr. Jarvey that Harry Blaney
had been unwilling to accept in public. . . . " I beg your
pardon?"

"I said," the clerk commented, "I don't know exactly
what Execulit does."

"I hope there's nothing wrong, Mr. Thatcher," Miss Fellows could not keep from chirping.

"No, no. And thank you."

The teller did not seem surprised by Thatcher's warmth;
he could not realize that his composure had been a tonic.

Making his way out, Thatcher stopped by Henley's office
to remark offhandedly that the teller appeared to be a
competent and intelligent youth, thus throwing the floor manager into a frenzy of half-sentences, suppositions, and apologies, and proceeded into the lobby bound for the elevators,
the sixth floor, and the work he had promised himself.

Again he stopped short—and at the Sloan nobody protested—then suddenly turned to go out onto the street. He
looked at 15 Broad for a moment, then with an impetuosity
that he would have been the first to censure, set out for Execulit, Incorporated.

It was housed, on the thirty-fourth floor, in considerable
style. The waiting room, a symphony in soothing beige,
boasted a secretary to match.

"You don't have an appointment?" she asked pleasantly,
but with definite appraisal in her eye.

"No." Thatcher wondered briefly how to frame his question. It was a little absurd to simply ask what Execulit did,
here in its opulent quarters. He should have asked Trinkam,
who could be relied on to know the blonde if he didn't know
Execulit. "I wanted . . ."

"What was your name, please?"

So bland was her well-modulated voice, that Thatcher
identified himself obediently, and before he could state his
purpose in coming, she had whisked herself out of sight. His
appearance must have passed whatever subtle tests existed,
because when she reappeared a few moments later, her
smile was a shade more welcoming.

"Mr. Jarvey will be able to fit you in," she told him. Just as his dentist's receptionist did.

She ushered him into Mr. Jarvey's office—this time a symphony in strong manly browns, with a piece of driftwood over a modern fireplace—and withdrew, leaving to him the problem of framing in an inoffensive way what he admitted to himself was unpardonable nosiness. He was wasting his time. The initiative was not to be his.

"Well, Mr. Thatcher," said Mr. Jarvey, rising from behind an incredible desk designed as a work of art by a thwarted Cubist, and coming to wring his hand. "Sit down, won't you? I'm very glad to see you." His voice was noticeably heartening, and he beamed reassuringly at Thatcher, who decided he had no alternative. He sat down.

"Er . . . yes. Mr. Jarvey, I confess I find this slightly embarrassing . . ."

Jarvey broke in with a low, musical laugh. "It always seems that way, of course, but you'll be surprised and pleased to discover how very efficient and businesslike our operations are. It's more or less the same thing—let's see, you're with the Sloan, aren't you?—well, it's the same thing as writing up a mortgage." He chuckled at his apt pleasantry.

The optimism also recalled his dentist to Thatcher. He smiled politely, and declined the box of Havanas that Mr. Jarvey was pushing toward him.

"No, thank you. I took the chance of coming up here, Mr. Jarvey, I must confess, on an impulse, and I'm not altogether sure . . ."

Jarvey sobered instantly. "It's often that way," he told Thatcher with a perplexing note of sympathetic understanding in his voice. "Sometimes it is a question of a fundamental, and often slow-developing sense of need. But quite frequently, it is, as you say, an impulse. Our position is that explorations are not necessarily binding—and so many people reject the notion of even considering what you have in mind because they don't realize this—but that they are well worth launching because the possibility of rewards—and I know that you are concerned primarily with nonmonetary rewards as well as the more humdrum—or should I say bread-and-butter?—aspects of what we can do."

He leaned back, pleased with himself, and awaited Thatcher's comment.

"Quite so. Now, Mr. Jarvey . . ." Thatcher temporized. He recognized a speech when he heard one, but he had rarely derived so little information from such fluent communication.

"Perhaps, Mr. Thatcher," Jarvey said insinuatingly, "Perhaps it would be smoother if I took over." He carefully adjusted his merriment to low gear. "I know that a man in your position has become accustomed to taking command of the situation. But I know you'll agree that, when you go to a specialist, you put yourself in his hands."

Thatcher, who never went to specialists, agreed that he did.

"Well, then, perhaps the first thing we should get out of the way is this: how long have you been at the Sloan?"

When you are being swept along by a raging torrent, it is easier to surrender to the tide rather than struggle against it. Unless, of course, there are rapids ahead. Thatcher could see no precipices in sight, and he liked to enlarge his experience.

"Let me see," he said, settling down comfortably in his chair. "I came to the Sloan in 1925 . . ."

"Nineteen twenty-five? Well, that's good and bad," Jarvey said quickly.

"You're right," Thatcher agreed gravely.

"And when . . . no, let's not beat around the bush. When did you first feel that you were becoming . . . let's say, dissatisfied at the Sloan? Or perhaps tired, is a better way to put it . . ."

"In 1927," Thatcher said.

Jarvey started slightly, but Thatcher continued in reflective tones. "I fought it, but the feeling recurred in 1936 . . ."

"Mr. Thatcher . . ."

"In the fall of 1946 I had some distressing symptoms . . ."

"Mr. Thatcher!"

"Mr. Jarvey, I must apologize." It was Thatcher's turn to

be warmly understanding. "We've been talking at cross-purposes, and wasting your valuable time. I am not trying to move from the Sloan. On the contrary, I came up here to inquire about an executive that I believe you are . . . ah . . . relocating."

Jarvey, hovering between outrage and amusement, briefly recalled the Sloan's last financial statement, and opted for amusement. He laughed fruitily. "Well," he said when he had finally, and with no discernible difficulty, recaptured his self-control, "It is an amusing misunderstanding, isn't it? But if you do try to find another position, Mr. Thatcher, I hope that you will come to Execulit. We do some very interesting work for men who are already at the top, but are still trying to find a challenge in their work. Now, who was it . . ."

Thatcher, who had foreseen the request for some information, was ready and fluent, as well as flattering, with his untruthful reply as to the source of his knowledge about Execulit.

"I've heard some very good reports about your executive placement service," he said, Disraeli to Jarvey's Victoria. "And I've heard rumors that Harry Blaney might be looking around. It seemed reasonable, with the troubles that they're having at National Calculating. As I said, it was on an impulse that I came up. And I'm sorry to say I was caught up in the spirit of your very able and convincing remarks . . ."

"Yes," Jarvey said with satisfaction. "You can see how the mistake occurred. We do a sort of custom-tailoring service"—and Thatcher recognized another of his little pleasantries—"in executive placement. We really counsel with our clients, discuss their industrial experience, analyze their wants and needs. Only then do we try to place them, and of course we undertake just as serious a study of the firms they may be joining. We don't look upon ourself as an employment service"—and he said it with distaste—"but as specialists in the placement of executives. Naturally, when you came in . . ."

"Tell me, what would you have done if I did want to leave the Sloan after thirty-seven years?" Thatcher wanted to know.

Jarvey cocked his head roguishly, as if the question held more than Thatcher had intended. "Ah-ha! Well, we would have referred you to some of our specialists . . ."

"Specialists?"

"Industrial psychiatrists, sociologists—and our Rorschach man, of course, to find out the kind of person you really are. We run tests, then ask you to come in for three or four weeks of intensive analysis. It isn't your past, but your future that counts, you know."

Again Thatcher recognized the speech, but this time he nodded encouragingly, and Jarvey flowed on. "Then, once we had really found the real you, we would turn to the problem of where you wanted to locate yourself. We would try to find a place that provided a challenge to your best creative talents . . ."

"What about money?"

Jarvey was pained. "We arrange a suitable fee based on your new salary, of course. But I do want to make clear that, only after we had really learned about you, would we start approaching companies. We have an extended dossier on them, but we would want to be sure that there was no change. Firms have a personality, you know . . ."

"I know . . ."

"So you see," Jarvey wound up, "we rarely if ever have a prospective employer approaching us. It's a more complex operation."

"I can see that," Thatcher said truthfully. "And Harry Blaney . . .?"

"Well, in confidence, I will say that Mr. Blaney has been one of our clients for over a month . . ."

"So I heard," Thatcher murmured absently, his thoughts elsewhere. If Blaney had been involved with Execulit for over a month, a substantial portion of the motive imputed to him by Richter disappeared. He certainly wasn't going to murder to protect a position in a firm he was leaving.

"There's been a leak," Jarvey said austerely, making a note of it. "Well, since you know, I can tell you that we have been working with Mr. Blaney, and I have no hesitation in telling you that he's really a first-rate man. These difficulties at National Calculating have created some problems, you know, but I think we will have no trouble in overcoming them. I tell you this, and I don't think I can say more unless the Sloan would be definitely interested. At any event, Mr. Thatcher, I don't think that the Sloan . . ." He let the sentence trail off.

"You're not sure that the Sloan would measure up to your standards?" Thatcher said.

Pleased with this ready comprehension, Jarvey nodded rather sadly. "I don't like to say it, Mr. Thatcher, but we haven't done much in the banking field. We feel, among other things, that its compensations are not the sort to encourage top-flight men—you see, I believe in complete frankness. We might consider putting the Sloan on our A-list, sometime in the future but at the moment . . . I'm sorry."

Thatcher rose. "I hope you'll reconsider that," he said with utmost seriousness. "I think I can safely say that I'd be most interested in anything you could suggest . . ."

Jarvey permitted himself a small smile. "We'll just have to see, Mr. Thatcher," he said rising. "But it has been a pleasure."

How rarely, thought Thatcher, as he smiled at the blonde and descended to the street, how rarely are those words true. It had indeed been a pleasure.

And it had been informative. Harry Blaney, while revealing symptoms of premature senility by falling into Exculit's manicured talons, was nonetheless now revealed as someone whose role at National Calculating had been persistently misinterpreted.

And if his behavior was no longer highly suspicious, it might be true that his testimony and disinterestedness were no longer suspect. Thatcher absentmindedly hailed a cab. Certainly if Harry Blaney was trying to leave National Calculating, and had been so planning even before Clarence Fortinbras hove into view, he might have some interesting comments on subsequent developments.

"Southern Bourbon Building."

He would wash his hands of National Calculating tomorrow.

# 16

## *Adieu, Adieu!*

He was soon receiving the warmest welcome he had yet experienced at National Calculating.

"Come in, come in," invited Blaney cordially as Thatcher hovered irresolutely on the threshold. "Glad to see you."

Blaney was the picture of confidence, serenity, and good cheer. Nodding benignly to the secretary who sat by his desk with her notebook flat against her knee, he said, "That's all for now, Janice. Would you type up that rough draft right away and let me see it? We should get it out today."

Thatcher settled himself while the secretary, gathering up his hat and coat, left the room and closed the door behind her. He decided to come straight to the point. With the slightly conspiratorial air appropriate to any executive discussion of job-hunting, he leaned forward and invested his tone with heavy significance.

"I bumped into Jarvey today. He tells me you're one of his clients."

"Yes. Just going off his list, as a matter of fact. Great little shop he runs, isn't it?" Blaney was totally unabashed.

"Going off his list?"

"Didn't he tell you? Oh, he must be playing it close to the chest. I'm going to Southern Midwest Electric as executive vice president." A satisfied smile made its appearance. "Settled the whole thing at noon. I had lunch with their president, Jack Barnett, today. A great guy! He's thinking of

retiring in a year or two. We should work well together."
Blaney leaned back in his chair expansively.

Thatcher murmured suitable congratulations. "Does anybody here at National know yet?"

"Not yet. As a matter of fact, I was just dictating my resignation when you came in." Suddenly he grinned boyishly. "You know, I really *like* writing resignations. Too many people just dash them off. It takes a little work to get one just right. I think they should be dignified but sincere. Don't you?"

"Well, I don't really know. Now that you mention it, I've very rarely resigned from anything—except formal appointments like board chairmanships and committees—that sort of thing." Thatcher thought with some contentment of his long sojourn at the Sloan. "I'm afraid I tend to stay with things, you know," he said apologetically.

Blaney was impressed. "Now me, I'm a mover. This is my twelfth change since the war. Always enjoy it too. There's nothing like the first six months on a job. A new setup, new people, new ways of doing things. I get a bang out of it," he confided engagingly.

Thatcher decided that, if Blaney wanted to make confidences, they should not be wasted on a general discussion of the modern corporate executive and his urge to flight. Blaney could be a fruitful source of information. Furthermore, with the approaching severance of the ties that bound him to National Calculating and the relaxation induced by the knowledge that he was about to launch himself on a new career, Blaney might answer a few straight questions which would call for more disclosure than an employee wholeheartedly committed to the interests of National would care to make.

"Yes, I'm sure these changes must be stimulating. And, of course, the situation here has been rather difficult lately," said Thatcher cautiously.

"You're damn right it's been difficult," agreed Blaney readily. "Any business has its ups and downs, and you expect to be treated like a bungler if you have the bad luck to be around during one of the downs. But that's not what's going

on here. Things were bad enough before Fortinbras showed
up. You could just about hear them sharpening up their axes
to get rid of me. And since Fortinbras, it's been a question of
fraud and murder. Now that," he added reasonably, "is not
what you expect when you come to a company."

"No, but then you have to admit that things have been
rather odd here. There has been a murder. And perhaps
there has been fraud."

"I suppose you're right," said Blaney, rubbing the bald
spot which was usually carefully hidden by his thinning hair.
"I never have been able to figure this place out. It's been a
funny operation right from the start. Take those two plants
in New Jersey. I lose money and Rutledge makes it. I can
see how I do it, but I'm damned if I can see how he does it.
Oh, I know what people must be saying. Either I'm a thief
or a nincompoop. Well, I know I'm not a thief and, as for
the other—" he paused to glare defiantly at Thatcher—"I'd
like to see how young Hammond makes out after I'm gone.
Now that's another thing. Hammond! He and Richter have
been politicking around for the last six months. You get
something like that anywhere. But not this way. Hammond's
supposed to be my subordinate. But I never could get any
support from Mason in dealing with him. And of course Chip
was too blind to see where the politicking was leading until
the other day." Blaney snorted with disgust and started to
rummage around in his desk drawer. His hand emerged
with a cigar which he started to prepare in a leisurely fashion.

"Does Mason realize the position now? I'm a stranger to
the company, of course, but it has seemed as if Richter—and
Hammond perhaps—weren't particularly subtle." Thatcher
courteously declined a belated offer of a cigar.

"Oh, he knows now. Hammond had a talk with him after
that Plout woman left here the other day. Hard to tell how
he feels about it." Blaney watched a thin ribbon of blue
smoke make its way to the window. "I wouldn't be surprised
if Chip doesn't even make a fight of it. He's got money, you
know, and he's sick to death of National Calculating. What
kind of a president is that? Naturally if he can't be bothered

defending his own position, he isn't going to defend mine. But I'd still give a lot to know what's been going on here."

"Someone did say something about your being seen with one of National's suppliers," suggested Thatcher delicately.

"Oh? And left you to draw your own conclusions, I suppose," said Blaney, with a surprising absence of heat. "Sure, I've been seeing a lot of Northfield Electronics. They're looking for a vice president. Offered it to me, actually, but I turned it down. We couldn't get together on a stock option, and the salary wasn't good enough without an option arrangement. No money changed hands," he added dryly.

It occurred to Thatcher that Blaney had been very active during the past six weeks. No wonder he had always been hurling himself into a coat, about to depart for an appointment. It would have required a good deal of movement to keep up a pretense of full-time absorption with the affairs of National Calculating and simultaneously to submit to Mr. Jarvey's schedule for prospective job applicants.

"You really have no idea of what's behind Fortinbras's murder?" he prodded. "Or for that matter this attack on young Draper?"

"What's that?" Blaney demanded. "I thought Draper had an accident." He raised his eyebrows. "You mean that that's why the police have been asking everybody where they were last night?"

"Yes, I think so . . ."

"Excuse me," said Blaney's secretary from the doorway. "I have that draft typed if you want to look it over, Mr. Blaney."

"Fine, fine," declared that enthusiastic resigner. "Bring it right in, Janice. Mr. Thatcher knows all my secrets."

The secretary laid the draft on the desk and prepared to leave.

"No, don't go. You don't mind, do you, Thatcher? This will just take a minute, and I want to give it to Chip Mason as soon as possible."

Thatcher agreed. With some amusement he watched Blaney lose himself in the problems of prose composition. A word was crossed out here, a substitution was effected somewhere else, and, after a few moments of frowning study, a lengthy addition was made at the bottom of the page.

"Here, listen to this, Thatcher, and tell me what you think of it. It may be a little too formal."

"Certainly. Go right ahead."

DEAR SIR:

This letter will serve as notice of my resignation from the position of vice president and division manager for Commercial Sales of National Calculating Corporation, such resignation to take effect immediately.

It has been a pleasure to be associated with National Calculating and to have the privilege of working with its fine management. I know that my years at National have provided me with a splendid opportunity to enrich my experience and develop my talents, and I hope that I have made some contribution in my turn.

For your information, it is my intention to take up the position of executive vice president at Southern Midwest Electric, Incorporated. I trust that this post will yield an opportunity for frequent contacts with all those colleagues with whom I have worked and whom I have come to admire. I shall continue to look back on our association with pleasure and gratitude.

Sincerely yours,

"There now, what do you think of it? Warm enough?" asked Blaney anxiously.

"Very warm . . . in fact, almost passionate."

"You're joking," said Blaney dubiously. He proceeded to reread his resignation, this time silently. He had been only too truthful when he said that he liked to take pains with the composition of his resignations. Of course, it explained all those job changes. If a man really enjoyed writing resignations and starting new jobs, the temptation to move and to move frequently must be irresistible. What would happen if the current president of this Southern Midwest fulfilled Blaney's expectations and retired after a decent interval, leaving Blaney as his heir apparent? Would Blaney be trapped into permanence? Would he become a secret resignation-writer? For that matter, what prompted a large utility to go out and hire as its president-elect a man in Blaney's present position—that is, manager of a notoriously unsuccessful division and possibly murder suspect into the bargain? It was done all the time, that Thatcher knew. Was it the selling power of Execulit? Or more simply, the unobtainability of successful men? He shook his head. The ways of modern business seemed very strange to a banker. Preserving a rigid silence out of respect for Blaney's creative endeavors, Thatcher continued to ponder the problem. Why, for instance, did a utility go to a computer business in search of its executives? Banks were admittedly old-fashioned, but Thatcher had been reared in the belief that the way to become a banker was to train as a banker. The prevailing philosophy these days seemed to be that a management elite existed. A cadre of men trained in principles so broad that they could leap with the merriest abandon from the communications industry to the automobile industry to the steel industry. Any day now, he thought glumly, one would hear of IBM raiding the management pool at the A&P.

Blaney had finally satisfied himself with a few last-minute insertions. "All right, Janice. Take it along and type it up. I'll deliver it personally as soon as you're done."

Janice departed silently.

"A great girl," said Blaney in his new charity for the entire personnel of National Calculating. "Knows how to keep her mouth shut too. I don't have to worry about the whole office gabbing before I can get up to see Mason." He was happily ignorant of the fact that Janice had already told the entire secretarial staff of his forthcoming departure. The secretaries, true to their trust, would never have dreamed of discussing the matter with their superiors until official notification of the event. So, in a sense, Blaney was right. The people who ought not to know would not know until Mason made some appropriate announcement. These things have a way of adjusting themselves.

"Well, I won't take up any more of your time, Blaney. I imagine that you have a lot to do," said Thatcher, rightly taking this reference to Mason as a subtle hint.

"Yes, I want to get all packed this afternoon. And Mason will want all the current information on Commercial Sales." He chuckled for a moment. "Hammond's been so busy with his politics for the last two or three weeks, that he hasn't paid much attention to the division. He's going to have to buckle down to some hard work for a change."

"For a man who has just written a touching encomium to the management of this company, you don't seem to have much personal affection for them," said Thatcher with some tartness.

Blaney waved vaguely. "You've got to be able to get along with anybody and everybody in business. And I can. But that doesn't mean you have to like them. Look at this company. Not a really decent human being in the place. That is, with the exception of Margaret Cobb. I'll admit that she is a really nice person. Look at the way she's been calling the hospital about young Draper. But what has she gotten out of it? Having a miserable little runt like Richter run in on top of her. Pah! Anyway, that reminds me. I want to say goodbye to Margaret. If you're going, I'll come down the corridor with you. Her office is right after the receptionist."

Thatcher, after a momentary hesitation, allowed himself to be swept along by Blaney's enthusiasm. Mrs. Cobb was a very elusive person, and it was high time that he had a talk with her. Just as well that he could be ushered in under cover of Blaney's news. She might well know a good deal more about the hidden affairs of National Calculating than anybody realized.

Whether she could be induced to part with this information was something else again.

# 17

## *Warlike Volley*

Every firm has its old regulars. There are one or two to be found even in those corporations most addicted to entrusting the guidance of their affairs to more conspicuous talents. And while the old regulars do not achieve the same status or the same financial rewards as their virtuosi brethren, they do have a way of digging themselves in and surrounding themselves with creature comforts—they get the office copy of the *Wall Street Journal* earlier than anybody else, their secretaries bring them home-brewed coffee in china cups instead of drugstore coffee in cardboard mugs, and staff dinners are held on Thursday nights because they have made it known that Wednesday is inconvenient for them.

As Thatcher entered Mrs. Cobb's office for the first time, he instinctively catalogued her as a very special sort of old regular. Her office was second in size only to that of Chip Mason. Its decoration differed just enough from that of the remainder of the executive suite to make a distinctive and suitable background for her thin, erect figure clad in a soft beige suit. The walls were covered with grass cloth, and several pieces of furniture in a honey-colored wood stood on a carpet of old gold. A small table by her desk held a spray of flowers and a cigarette box of French china.

It was not until they had actually advanced into the room in order to allow Harry Blaney to take a fond farewell of

Mrs. Cobb and a heartily insincere farewell of Jay Rutledge, who was ensconced in a deep chair on the other side of the desk, that Thatcher received his second impression. He and Blaney had interrupted a quarrel. Or perhaps "difference of opinion" would better describe the disagreement which seemed to have arisen between the two most reserved personalities in the front office of National Calculating. This was apparent, during Blaney's short stay, only from the punctilious formality of their references to each other. They both avoided direct address.

"So you're leaving, Harry. Well, that's a shame," drawled Rutledge, "but this deal you've got at Southern Midwest sounds too good to pass up. I'm sure Margaret agrees."

"Commercial Sales won't be the same without you, Harry," sighed Mrs. Cobb. "We'll miss you. I know Jay feels the same."

"You haven't told Chip yet? It will be a body blow to him. This is a ticklish time to give Hammond more authority, but he won't have any choice. Someone has to run the division. Margaret's always said that Chip didn't realize Hammond had his eye on the presidency, and not by inheritance either."

Mrs. Cobb was not to be outdone in these pretty shows of deference. "Allen's been thinking along these lines for a long time. But he knows it won't work without Jay. And Jay can't be pressured because he doesn't have to side with anyone. His position is a lot more solid than anybody else's."

And so the ritual rhythm of response and antiphon continued until Blaney remembered that he still had to see Mason, and rushed off with parting words of encouragement and advice about the big management struggle which his resignation would surely trigger. The diversion over, Rutledge and Mrs. Cobb returned to the main issue so quickly that Thatcher had no opportunity to apologize for his continued presence.

"You know I don't like to complain, Margaret," rumbled Rutledge, settling down to complain at length. "But when I asked Chip to lift some of the load of entertaining Cartwright, I thought I was going to be helped."

He paused meaningfully.

Mrs. Cobb raised an eyebrow.

It was apparent that they were both beyond recalling Thatcher.

"And you don't feel that my entertaining General Cartwright has been a help?"

"Just the opposite," said Rutledge bluntly.

Mrs. Cobb's lips tightened. She raised her eyes from the pad on which she was doodling a complicated pattern, and looked at her colleague coldly.

"You know, Jay, you haven't yet told me exactly what it is you're complaining about. Do you think you could overcome your well-known dislike of complaining to that extent?"

Rutledge ignored this provocation. "Now, Margaret," he said placatingly, "let's not get upset about this. I don't really like to bring it up, but Cartwright is an important customer, and we're all concerned that he's handled properly."

Mrs. Cobb's voice took on a steely quality. Thatcher began to understand how she had managed to maintain her position at National Calculating. It would not be at all easy for a Morris Richter to win a round from Margaret Cobb. He bent forward with interest. It might even be beyond the powers of a Jay Rutledge.

"I'm waiting for you to tell me exactly how I handled him improperly."

"All right," said Rutledge grimly. "Since you insist on it. You were supposed to take Cartwright out, help him relax, show him some hospitality. You weren't supposed to give him your ideas on how my division should be run."

Poor Cartwright! If this was Rutledge's reaction, how must the General feel about it, thought Thatcher. All day spent getting Rutledge's views on National Calculating, then all night getting Mrs. Cobb's. Before he had finished his stay in New York, he would be looking back to the Battle of the Bulge as a halcyon period of rest and repose.

"Stop overstating things, Jay," said Margaret Cobb in distinct rebuke. The remark was calculated to annoy, and it succeeded.

"Don't take that tone with me," he said sharply. "You

should know better than to intrude into areas where you're not professionally competent. You're in research and development, not in production."

"Not professionally competent! I know more about laminated circuits than you'll ever know."

Thatcher was entranced. He had wondered if there were any possibility of breaking through Margaret Cobb's icy reserve, and it looked as if the job was going to be done for him. The lady was not far from shouting with rage.

"On a drawing board, maybe," admitted Rutledge slowly, looking apologetically toward Thatcher. He obviously regretted stinging himself and his colleague into an open display of hostility before the banker. "But not," he concluded stubbornly, "not on a production line. Look here, Margaret, I didn't mean to offend you. But you know perfectly well that this is no time to be throwing difficulties in the way of the new contract. Cartwright's already been shocked at the situation here. Stockholder suits, outside audits, and then Fortinbras's death."

The olive branch was summarily rejected. No scientist likes to be told that his (or her) competence lies in the world of the abstract, that when harsh reality must be confronted he should go away with his toys and let the adults cope with the situation.

"I don't care what you meant! What you're saying is that I don't know enough to talk to General Cartwright about circuits that were developed under *my* direction. If you think for one minute that I'll permit you to exercise this kind of control over my activities you're in for a big surprise. I will say and do precisely what I please! You can run your tame general through hoops if you want to, but you'll have to keep him on a leash if you intend to protect him from my professional incompetence. And we'll take that right up to Mason, Cartwright, and the Joint Chiefs of Staff if you want to make an issue of it!" Mrs. Cobb's voice was now a thoroughly alarming basso profundo that rocked the room with its vehemence. She had risen to her feet and was facing Rutledge over her desk defiantly.

"I do not want to make an issue of it!" said Rutledge with patent sincerity. "But I'm not going to have a seventy-million-dollar contract whistled down the wind just because you can't control your tongue."

"I can control anything I want to, including my job," retorted his old friend. "You're not doing such a good job of selling Cartwright if you're this nervous. This is the first time you've even mentioned losing the contract. Up to now, you've been telling us there was nothing to worry about. It was as good as signed. If you ask me, you don't think you're going to be able to sell Cartwright, and you're looking for a whipping boy. Where would you be without this contract?"

"I never had any trouble selling this contract until you started butting in! And, by God, I'm beginning to wonder if it was so accidental. Have you thrown in with Richter and Hammond? I'll warn you right now, you won't be able to edge me out." Rutledge had sobered himself out of his rage and was eying his opponent suspiciously.

"I don't have to throw in with anybody. And I don't have to let anybody walk over me either."

"All right, all right," said Rutledge impatiently. "Nobody's trying to. Just stay in your own garden. I've got enough to worry about without your giving misinformation to Cartwright."

"It wasn't misinformation!" Mrs. Cobb was prepared to fire up again.

"I don't care what it was," growled Rutledge. "Leave Cartwright to me, that's all."

Thatcher noted that it was the lanky Southerner who was anxious to avoid a reopening of hostilities. A referee would have had no hesitation in awarding the bout to Mrs. Cobb on a technical knockout. Clearly the lady's position at National Calculating was a strong one if she could take on Jay Rutledge concerning a matter which, while by no means clear to Thatcher, seemed to have reference to the operation of Rutledge's division. On her own ground, she must be even more formidable. It would be interesting to see Morris Richter trying to give her orders. Thatcher suspected that the situation simply did not arise. Richter, if he remembered properly, showed a rather startling loyalty to Mrs. Cobb. No doubt he had learned that that was the way to survive.

Meanwhile Mrs. Cobb was savoring the fruits of her triumph. She subjected her late antagonist to a thoughtful inspection. After a moment's silence, she spoke quietly.

"You know what the trouble is, Jay?" she remarked in conversational tones. "You want to keep everything to yourself. Just letting anybody know the total sales of your division is a terrible exposure to you."

"I don't know what you're talking about," said Rutledge deliberately, "and I don't much care either."

"It's true," she continued inexorably. "You want to keep everything a secret—your contracts, your generals, your books, and your plant."

"What do you mean—my books?" replied Rutledge, stung on a point which had become a battle cry at National Calculating since the advent of Clarence Fortinbras. "I'm perfectly willing to show my books to anyone. I don't have the kind of thing to hide that the rest of you do. I make profits, remember?" he drawled unkindly.

"That's what makes it so strange." Mrs. Cobb still spoke in a mildly reflective mood, but Thatcher had seen the danger signals once and knew she was again on the verge of losing her temper.

"You're mad!" said Rutledge quietly. "I was the one who persuaded Chip to go through with the Sloan's audit. I've been ready to show my books to anyone."

"Not to Clarence, you weren't!"

Mrs. Cobb put her hand to her mouth in a sudden uncharacteristic movement of confusion. But Rutledge and Thatcher had both heard her unguarded slip. They stiffened instantly.

"Oh, it's Clarence, is it?" It was Rutledge's turn to be thoughtful. "You know, I always wondered how come he was so knowledgeable. There just had to be an inside tipster who was slipping him scandal. But I never thought of you, Margaret; I didn't realize you were capable of that sort of thing. I suppose it's because you got tired waiting all these years for some kind of success, some kind of recognition."

Rutledge shook his head. He rose.

"Wait, Jay." Mrs. Cobb stretched out an impulsive hand. "I can explain everything."

"I'm sure you can," said Rutledge sadly from the door. "You always do, don't you? But this time I don't want to hear."

He turned and left the room slowly, but very surely.

# 18

# *Lady-in-Waiting*

It was a moment before the silence was broken. "I don't know what's come over Jay Rutledge," Mrs. Cobb said in a voice that retained its edge.

Thatcher turned his eyes from the door. Like her, he had been taken aback by the uncharacteristic offensiveness which Rutledge had brought to the argument, and by the implacability of his exit; Mrs. Cobb's comment reminded him that normally she was the most self-possessed of women. Yet her exchange with Rutledge had been heated, and even now she was in the grip of an emotion that disturbed her habitual, rather glacial composure.

As he watched, she took a deep breath and sat down at her desk, her lips tightly compressed.

"I'll be getting out of your way," he said apologetically. Although he had taken no part in the dispute, he felt the embarrassment natural to a man who, however innocently, has become involved in a free-for-all.

Mrs. Cobb ignored his comment, and continued to stare at the door through which Jay Rutledge had taken his dramatic exit. "I simply do not understand him," she repeated. "Jay is normally the most balanced and sane person at National. It's so completely out of character for him to cast aspersions, and walk off in this preposterous manner . . ." She let the sentence trail off and shrugged her shoulders to punctuate it; but clearly she was not through with John

Thatcher, who waited for the return of her attention with some uneasiness.

He rather thought she wanted to talk to him without knowing quite how to begin, and if Mrs. Cobb wanted to talk, John Thatcher was willing to oblige. "Of course, his position is a little awkward. I gather that he and Mr. Fortinbras didn't hit it off . . ." he suggested.

She stopped him with a look of almost paralyzing intelligence. "You heard Jay, Mr. Thatcher," she said, quietly mocking. "Surely you realize that he was accusing me of hiding some more sinister connection with Clarence. And I did call him Clarence! That's very suspicious, don't you think?"

Thatcher bowed his head, accepting reproof. The low level of intelligence obtaining generally at National Calculating had led him to make the error of treating Mrs. Cobb as if she were the mental equal of Chip Mason.

"Well, I can allay any suspicions you may have," she continued with a wry smile. "There's no reason to hide it now. Clarence Fortinbras was my brother-in-law."

In-laws being such comic sorts of relations, Thatcher was conscious of a start of amused anticlimax, which he prudently suppressed. And in his silence, Mrs. Cobb continued, in a musing voice. "He married my sister Emily. When he told me about his descent on National Calculating, he suggested that it might embarrass me, or put me in a difficult position. I told him that I didn't mind in the least—and frankly, National needs me more than I need National—but he insisted. So we simply didn't publicize the fact of our relationship." She stared bleakly into space for a moment. "And that's all that Jay's sinister suggestions are worth!"

Thatcher braced himself not to be intimidated by this formidable woman. "Well, that does explain a good many puzzling odds and ends, I confess."

She raised an eyebrow at him, and her eyes were almost too knowing, he thought. "As you yourself mentioned," he explained, "you called him Clarence once or twice. It gave rise to some questions in certain circles. Then—by George!"

he broke off as a sudden thought struck him. "Did Dr. Richter know that Fortinbras was related to you?"

She smiled openly at that. "Has Morris been protecting me? Yes, I rather think that he did stumble on the fact. He saw us lunching together one day, and Morris is terribly curious about things. He came into my office a little later and made a number of heavily significant remarks. At the time, I was too busy to humor him. Did he think that I might have killed Clarence?"

Thatcher temporized. "I think that he might have been afraid that you were . . . involved in some way. He's fond of you."

"Morris will be quite a nice person if he ever grows up," she said with absent affection but no undue respect for her chief. Thatcher was inclined to accept the assessment of both: Mrs. Cobb was quite capable of murder, and Richter would be quite nice when he grew up.

Mrs. Cobb frowned slightly as her thoughts moved elsewhere. "You know, Clarence was really a very sweet person. He and Emily were happy together for a long time." This was offered in a carefully emotionless voice. "I wouldn't want you to think that because I haven't mentioned my relationship to him, I haven't felt this murder very keenly. Or that I haven't tried to do what I can to find out why it happened."

Thatcher assumed a look of grave sympathy, and reflected that he would not like to have Mrs. Cobb tracking him down; there was a rather frightening detachment about her. She held her slight body no more than energetically erect, but he had a sudden impression of a majestically tall, iron-willed figure of retribution, ready to plumb the depths of the mystery that surrounded Clarence Fortinbras's death.

". . . and around here, of course, he was looked upon as an eccentric. I admit that he was hot-tempered, and occasionally self-willed. But that is not unusual in men who have spent their lives in academic surroundings. And Clarence had made a great name for himself as a brilliant accountant. But he was more than that. He was an extremely intelligent, reasonable man." She broke off and looked intently at Thatcher.

"He impressed me very favorably when we met," he replied, wondering if the remark sounded patronizing.

"Some people were inclined to think that he . . . he was a bit of a clown." It was a question, not a statement.

"Oh, I don't believe anybody who met him and talked seriously with him was in any danger of underestimating his remarkable intelligence," Thatcher said, wondering why Mrs. Cobb needed reassurance on the point.

She told him. "I'm glad that you feel that way," she said. "Because if you didn't I wouldn't say what I'm going to say. The staff at National Calculating and the police have dismissed him as a sort of pest, and I'm not sure that they would take my comments seriously."

"Comments?"

"Clarence was very close-mouthed about his work," Mrs. Cobb began, then she smiled, revealing the woman who lurked behind the forbidding public personage who was Dr. Margaret Cobb. "I know that he seemed to be a nosy person, but when it came to things that really count—his work, for example—he was very reticent. He didn't confide in me, and I didn't ask him to. But since he knew I was interested, he occasionally let things drop."

Thatcher felt the stirrings of interest. "Did he tell you what he was doing?" he demanded baldly.

"He said that he felt he was going to find something more important than ineptitude at National Calculating. God knows, there's plenty of that. But Clarence said that he had uncovered a fraudulent scheme." Mrs. Cobb looked across the desk at Thatcher. "He said he had rarely seen such artistry in fraud."

Tribute indeed, thought Thatcher. Aloud, he said, "I thought it must be something like that." He turned over in his mind the information he had been given about National Calculating: Harry Blaney and his disappointing Commercial Sales, Jay Rutledge's profitable Government Contracts, Table Model's slow and steady growth, Research and Development which had produced nothing. Plenty of elbow room for fraud, but what kind? Fortinbras was so superior an accountant that it was not only possible, it was likely that his thorough and punitive methods would uncover something that the ordinary accountant, using the ordinary accounting methods, might miss. Thatcher truly valued Addison, but he knew that he lacked the Fortinbras demon.

"He said," Mrs. Cobb continued with great care, "he said that he thought only a physical inventory could confirm his guess. Then he said that it would be as big a scandal as the old McKesson-Robbins case. I don't know what that was, but I do remember that it was McKesson-Robbins."

She looked hopefully at him, and Thatcher, puzzling over the late Clarence Fortinbras's remarks, had a tiny but not uninteresting revelation: Mrs. Cobb was talking to him not because she was shaken by her encounter with Jay Rutledge, and far less because she wanted a comforting shoulder. She was consulting him, as coolly as she would consult a mathematician, for professional advice. Margaret Cobb did not understand what her brother-in-law had told her; she felt the police would fail to make use of her information as she felt it should be used. Therefore, she was deliberately consulting Thatcher as a man likely to be interested and, more important, professionally knowledgeable about financial and accounting details.

It was a sobering thought, and she confirmed it explicitly. "I don't know what Clarence meant," she said, "and I thought that you would." There was a simple finality about her statement, but no humility. Margaret Cobb knew what she knew, and knew what she did not know.

"I think I understand what he meant," Thatcher said slowly. "Or rather, I think I have a vague idea. But I'm not the accountant that Fortinbras was, and it will take a little research . . ."

She did not press him. Having reported her information to the proper authorities (as she saw them), Margaret Cobb was prepared to trust them. Thatcher began to feel the burden of that trust.

The message transmitted, Mrs. Cobb let her eyes stray

meaningfully back to the pile of documents in her in-basket. Thatcher obediently took the hint, and made his departure.

Outside of her office, he stood for a moment, then, for no particular reason, expelled a sigh of relief. Mrs. Cobb often had this effect on her male colleagues.

Not for a moment did Thatcher believe that she had hidden her relationship with Clarence Fortinbras for any reason but the one she had explained. Although her personality was powerful enough to embrace a capacity for murder, her response to Fortinbras's death left no doubt about her innocence. Or no doubt with him. Possibly it was merely the forcefulness that surrounded her.

His opinion of Morris Richter went up a few notches. If that young man could work with Mrs. Cobb, and incur nothing more than her mild contempt, if he could ferret out secrets that she was trying to keep, then there was more to him than met the eye.

And, as Mrs. Cobb had remarked, Morris Richter was curious. Having indulged himself so far, Thatcher decided to go whole hog and pump Richter.

He turned the corner to Dr. Richter's offices, and passing through an empty secretary's cubicle, knocked on the door.

"Come in," Richter's resonant baritone replied.

His luck held. Richter was in conference with General Cartwright, and they greeted him with flattering cordiality.

"I don't want to interrupt," he said, "but I thought I'd come by to catch my breath. I've just been party to a nasty disagreement between Mrs. Cobb and Rutledge, and I wanted to get some details . . ."

"Well, now," General Cartwright interrupted with a grin. "That must have been a real shindig. Isn't Mrs. Cobb something? You know, we had a little difference of opinion the other night, and she as good as told me that I didn't know my business." He let his grin broaden admiringly. "The only people who tell me that sort of thing nowadays are congressmen, you know. And Mrs. Cobb." It seemed to have made a great hit with him.

Richter smiled, but Thatcher thought he detected constraint. It was all too obvious that Mrs. Cobb must have favored him with her opinion of his work at one time or another.

"What were you arguing about, General?" he asked.

"Well, I don't want to bore you . . ."

"Oh, you're not boring me."

Cartwright looked up at him, then shrugged slightly. "We were on our way out to the Boat Show on Long Island. Calvin Cobb is a lawyer, but he's interested in boats, and I am too. And we got to talking about one thing and another . . ."

Thatcher tried to control his impatience; having fallen into General Cartwright's arms, so to speak, and having unearthed some information that piqued his curiosity, he felt it behooved him to contain himself and wait out the General's diffuseness of manner. Richter, he noticed, was eying him curiously. No fool, young Richter.

". . . then about the TCR. I don't know why, but I mentioned the fact that I told Jay we hoped you people in Research and Development would figure out a way to make them last a little longer than one year. I guess I shouldn't have done that instead of going through channels, but you know, when you have to go up to the Hill to justify an annual budget of over fifty million dollars . . ."

"One year?" Richter repeated.

The General let a shade of sternness cross his boyish face. "Now don't tell me that I'm going to have to go through the same thing with you!"

Richter opened his mouth to reply, but Thatcher overruled him.

"Tell me about your discussion with Mrs. Cobb," he said firmly.

Imperceptibly the atmosphere in the office had altered; with a frown the General looked first at Richter, then at Thatcher. Rejecting the question that rose to his lips, he replied in a much more sober voice. "I told Mrs. Cobb that when the TCR wears out, we ship it to National Calculating for a trade-in . . ."

"But not in one year!" Richter could not keep from protesting.

The General's sternness became pronounced. "Seems to me

you people don't know what you're doing with both hands," he snapped. "Don't you know how Rutledge's contract reads? Sure, we ship them in for a trade-in . . ."

"And you get credit toward a new one," Richter interrupted, bringing a real scowl to the General's brow. "But not each year. You must have made a mistake . . ."

Diplomatically, Thatcher intervened. "What did Mrs. Cobb say, General?" he asked. Light was beginning to dawn, and to judge from Richter's horrified expression, Thatcher was not alone.

General Cartwright again abandoned Richter. "Well, I told her we never got more than one year's wear out of a TCR on range use." He paused for a moment, to let the military certainty of his remark sink in on their consciousness, then resumed his easy, off-duty manner. "And do you know what Mrs. Cobb said? She said I was all wrong." He chuckled genially, although Richter's remark along those lines had not visibly delighted him. "Had quite a set-to with her. I will say that she certainly sounds convincing. And nice as she is, there's no budging her, is there? Nothing would make her admit that the TCR doesn't last about a year . . ."

"I should think not," Richter said grimly. "And she's completely right!"

# 19

# The Clash of Arms

There was a pregnant pause during which General Cartwright gathered his forces for a knockout punch. He underestimated the nervous—but positive—volubility of his opponent.

"We know about them, General, even though they're Government Contracts products and we aren't encouraged to do much with them. Harry Blaney asked us if we could develop a small Information Storage Unit—one that he could sell separately to the trade. You know that the ISU that goes into military hardware operates under much more stringent conditions . . ."

What was needed here, Thatcher realized, was a steady guiding hand. Irritated though he was, the General could not resist any discussion of the TCR.

". . . heavier and probably more sensitive than you would want in commercial use," Richter was continuing earnestly.

"Yes, we have to have pretty narrow tolerances," Cartwright agreed.

"Yes," Thatcher said hastily. "Now, Dr. Richter, I take it that you are fairly familiar with the . . . the Information Storage Unit, was it? Would you tell me exactly . . ."

"The Target Control Release," said General Cartwright with a proprietary air that bespoke affection and pride, "is basically composed of two components . . ."

Richter, the scientist, winced.

". . . the Photoelectric Circuit is in effect the trigger, and the Information Storage Unit is what you might call the brain. It programs the information that it receives . . ."

"I see," Thatcher lied. "Tell me, how would you allocate costs?"

"Allocate costs?" repeated the General with severity. "Now what do you mean by that?"

The tone was calculated to depress the pretensions of impertinent junior officers, but the AEF was a long way behind John Thatcher, and he had never been impressionable.

"I mean that if a TCR costs four thousand dollars . . ."

"Some of them are as expensive as ten thousand dollars," said the General admiringly. "They're the ones we use to support the heavy artillery . . ."

"Yes, yes," Thatcher muttered, rubbing his chin. The task was not merely to unearth the facts he wanted; it also involved avoiding the flow of information that these specialists were eager to impart.

". . . beautiful," General Cartwright was saying with real feeling. "You know in the Louisiana Maneuvers last year we got 96 percent efficiency . . ."

"Ninety-six!" Richter exclaimed. "I hadn't realized that you had reached that level . . ."

Ruthlessly, Thatcher dragged them back to the question at issue. "Costs," he repeated bluntly. "How much of this four thousand dollars—or ten thousand dollars—would you say was the cost of the Photoelectric Circuit?"

"Oh, I see what you're getting at," Richter said.

Thatcher resisted the temptation to snarl. He waited. Richter frowned. "I'd say the Photoelectric Circuit could be replaced for—oh, let's say five hundred dollars. Of course, the bigger models . . ."

"Am I correct in inferring that the Photoelectric Circuit represents approximately 10 percent of the total cost of the TCR, and the Information Storage Unit accounts for the remaining 90 percent?" Thatcher demanded caustically. For men who grappled daily with knotty problems of national security and the farther reaches of modern mathematics,

Cartwright and Richter were surprisingly blank at this simple question.

Cartwright pulled himself together, a troubled expression on his handsome face. "You could say that," he admitted cautiously.

"Now this Information Storage Unit that accounts for roughly 90 percent of the costs of the TCR . . ."

"It's a complex unit, you understand," Richter interrupted. "It involves an extremely sensitive . . ."

"What about this disagreement?" Thatcher said bruskly. Beating around the bush would make him the world's authority on the TCR; but he was seeking different information. "The General says it wears out in a year, and you say it doesn't. Is that it?"

Both Cartwright and Richter were taken aback at this extremely abbreviated version of their quarrel, but once again Richter's verbal facility gave him the edge over his more weighty opponent. "Er . . . yes. As I was saying, Mrs. Cobb and I have worked with it for several months, testing it under operational conditions. We can prove that its expectation of life would be at least two years under normal military conditions." He was about to continue, but Thatcher turned to see how the General took his remarks.

He took them badly. "I don't know what's going on around here," he said grimly, "but I don't think I like it. I told Mrs. Cobb, and I'm telling you, and I'll tell anybody, that the United States Army uses a TCR for one year. And then it goes haywire!"

Thatcher digested this. He recognized authority when he heard it; he was prepared to believe that Richter and Mrs. Cobb had tested the TCR and found its life expectancy was two years, and that General Cartwright knew what he was talking about when he insisted that one year was all that the United States Army got out of it. If both of them were right, a rational explanation of the contradiction had some interesting implications.

Richter was, however, as Mrs. Cobb said, young for his age.

"You're sure you're not thinking of the Photoelectric Circuit alone, General?" he asked with a small and, Thatcher thought, ill-advised smile. "That would be virtually useless at the end of a year, but if you replaced it you should get another year out of the Information Storage Unit . . ."

"We don't," the General said flatly.

Richter was eager to find an excuse for the General's error. "Or possibly your installation practices aren't right. You know, if you don't adjust the calibration properly . . ."

"Our service personnel"—the General bit the words—"spend a two-week training period in National Calculating's TCR factory." He paused to let the words sink in. "Something's fishy here," he said, narrowing his eyes, "and I think we'd better get to the bottom of it."

Thatcher was delighted to enlist an ally; the ribbons adorning the General's tunic testified that he would be useful.

"I think I may be able to help you there," he said quietly.

"How?" Richter demanded unflatteringly.

Before Thatcher could answer, he was interrupted.

"Dr. Richter," said Mary Sullivan, appearing in the doorway. "We haven't got your quarterly estimates . . . Oh, I'm sorry." She stopped short at their forbidding looks. "I didn't mean to interupt."

Thatcher decided to abandon his normal courtesy for a show of force.

Without giving Richter a chance to reply, he said, "Will you come in and sit down, Miss Sullivan?"

Miss Sullivan advanced into the room, an amused but uncertain expression in her gray eyes.

"Do you want a secretary?" she asked, seeking an explanation for this peculiar behavior.

"We want information," Thatcher said grimly. He looked into her sensible eyes, and took a decision. "As you see, we're having a high-level conference, and I think you may be able to help us."

She waited. His opinion of her went up. "Needless to say this is . . . this is in strictest confidence." By which he meant he did not want this conversation reported back to Chip Mason unless necessary.

"Yes, I understand," Miss Sullivan replied with composure. Thatcher rather thought that she did.

"Now," he said, turning back to the combatants, "We have a contradiction here in your experiences with the life of the Information Storage Unit. It can be resolved easily enough —if the Army does get only one year's wear out of a device that Dr. Richter and Mrs. Cobb are professionally certain is longer-lived. It involves some very intricate"—he recalled Mrs. Cobb's quote—"and artistic fraud."

"Impossible!"

"Fraud! What are you talking about?"

"And," he continued implacably, "I might add, a very strong motive for murder."

He heard Miss Sullivan draw in her breath sharply but her face reflected thought, not shock.

"Now, General . . ."

"Yes sir," Cartwright said, instinctively responding to the unmistakable note of command.

"You were saying that you get one year out of the TCR. What happens to it then?"

The General was happy with matters of fact. "Under the terms of our last contract, we ship them in to National and get credited by some amount—usually from five hundred to one thousand dollars—this credit is used against our new purchases." He stopped, then like a man slowly beginning to realize the extent of damage, said, "My God! We must purchase over a thousand TCR's a month . . ."

"Where do they go?"

"Go?"

There was a blank silence for a moment. Cartwright looked accusingly about the room as the full possibilities of the situation began to emerge. Richter was playing nervously with a pencil, an unhappy frown on his normally confident face.

"Yes," persisted Thatcher, "I want to know exactly where —where in National Calculating, that is—these trade-ins go."

"I could call our Contract Liaison Officer and have him check with traffic control." Cartwright frowned his dissatisfaction. "But all this will take time. I want to settle this here and now!"

"Allen would know," Mary Sullivan volunteered. She reddened as everyone turned to her in surprise. "Allen Hammond," she explained. "He took a management orientation course when he first came to National, and he spent three months over in New Jersey at Government Contracts."

"Then let's get him in here," said the General crisply.

"But quietly," cautioned Thatcher. "There's no need to let the whole office know that something is brewing."

"No, indeed," agreed Richter with feeling. "After all, we don't know anything definite yet." He had the instincts, noted Thatcher dispassionately, of the rising company man.

"I'm sure Miss Sullivan is capable of detaching Mr. Hammond from his companions, whoever they are, with suitable discretion," Thatcher said blandly.

Mary Sullivan accepted this accolade with a gleam of suspicion, but rose to follow instructions.

"I'll bring him back right away if he's in the building," she assured them.

Richter looked knowing. "You can see which way the wind is blowing there," he said significantly.

A gloomy silence was his only answer. Thatcher disapproved of office gossip on general principles, and General Cartwright was exhibiting the single-minded tenacity of purpose which had evoked so much approval from his superiors in Korea. Richter sighed dispiritedly, and abandoned his attempts to lighten the atmosphere.

Mary Sullivan returned almost immediately with Hammond.

"Allen knows," she said on entering the room, "but he guessed why I asked."

"Naturally," said Thatcher dampeningly, "but there's no point in discussing our suspicions until we have some proof."

Allen Hammond was not offended. He had seated himself on the arm of Mary Sullivan's chair and was swinging one foot slowly as he examined the serious faces of the gathering.

"That's right," he agreed. "The trade-ins go to the Government Contracts warehouse at 1407-63 Fourth Street in Jersey City. The foreman at the warehouse is Joseph Bianchi. We have a tie line to the warehouse if you want to call."

Thatcher nodded approvingly. Hammond had imparted all the necessary information in a minimum of words without offering any speculations or protests. He also lacked the compulsive desire to convey irrelevant detail which made conversation with Richter and Cartwright so difficult. Perhaps it was simply a lack of intimate association with the TCR.

"Well, that isn't going to prove anything," said Richter. "The point is—"

"Exactly," interrupted Thatcher smoothly. "The point is, where do they go from there?"

"And we're going to find that out right now," announced Cartwright decisively. "There's going to be no cover-up."

Richter started to disclaim any such intention but Hammond quietly stepped into the picture.

"You can set your mind at rest on that point, General. If what we suspect is a fact, this is much too big to cover up." He regarded the tip of his brown oxford silently as if seeking inspiration. "Remember this is more than a matter of fraud. It's a matter of murder!"

"Then we're all agreed." Thatcher looked around for the nods of tacit confirmation. "This foreman can probably give us the information. But it occurs to me that it's time we resorted to some of Clarence Fortinbras's methods."

"Fortinbras?" The General's frown cleared. "Of course. This must be what he discovered. Well," he said impatiently, "what do you want to do?"

"The Sloan's accountant, Henry Addison, is here. I want to send him out to raid some files."

Richter and Hammond exchanged a long look.

"The records of Government Contracts have already been delivered to the accounting department for Mr. Addison to examine," said Hammond quietly.

"I know." Thatcher's voice was dry. "But I don't think that those records would be particularly informative. Perhaps Miss Sullivan wouldn't mind finding Henry Addison for us."

"No, you wait here, Mary." Hammond's hand rested on Mary Sullivan's shoulder for a moment. "I'll get him for you, sir. You're right. It's time we got this whole thing cleared up."

"I hope," said General Cartwright firmly as the door closed behind Hammond, "that young man hasn't got any foolish notions about going to see anybody else other than Addison."

"Certainly not," Mary Sullivan fired up. "Allen would never do such a thing, and you have no right to suggest that he would."

Startled by this unexpected attack, the General blinked, then smiled comprehendingly. "So that's what you meant," he said to Richter conversationally. "All the same, Miss Sullivan," he continued in a grim voice, "those records had better be there when this accountant of Mr. Thatcher's goes for them. I intend to place this whole affair in the hands of the Government Accounting Office, and they'll want documentary evidence."

"I don't think there will be any trouble about evidence now that we know what to look for, General," said Thatcher, preventing any misguided attempt on the part of the usually intelligent Mary Sullivan to come to grips with Cartwright. "The normal fraud is an attempt to cover up losses, not to explain profits. That's what has fooled the auditors up till now."

Cartwright nodded. "As I see it, all we're trying to do this afternoon is establish our suspicions."

"Yes," agreed Thatcher. "After that, a physical inventory will supply all the proof that you or the Government Accounting Office will need."

"All right." Richter cleared his throat, and resumed his professorial air. "Then we'd better make sure of exactly what we need to know to confirm your case. I don't want to go any further with this on the basis of vague suspicions."

Cartwright snorted. "Vague! It's you and Mrs. Cobb who've been so certain of your facts."

"Now, now. Dr. Richter agrees with us, I'm sure." Thatcher spoke quickly to prevent any further digressions into

the life expectancy of the TCR. "And for his satisfaction, I
think we need only two facts." He held up two fingers.

"We have to know what happens to the TCR when it
comes in as a trade-in, and the Photoelectric Circuit is
junked. In other words, what happens after the trade-ins
get to the warehouse in New Jersey. Right?" He slowly
lowered one of his upraised fingers. There was no disagreement.

"And we would like Henry Addison to take a look at the
accounts on the cost of the Information Storage Unit. Prefer-
ably before those records are prepared for examination by
an accountant."

Thatcher looked around the small group. Mary Sullivan
eyed his extended forefinger as if it were the raised blade
of a guillotine. Suddenly he snapped it down, and she shud-
dered.

Three hours later General Cartwright and John Thatcher
received reports from Henry Addison and from Joseph Bianchi who had been personally summoned from his duties at
the warehouse in New Jersey under conditions of great
secrecy. Allen Hammond and Morris Richter were both present, but Mary Sullivan had excused herself on the grounds
that even Charles Mason might begin to suspect something
if deprived of the presence of his secretary for four consecutive hours.

Curiously enough, however, she did not turn her steps to
the presidential office upon being released from proceedings which, under the direction of General Cartwright, were
assuming the character of a Military Court of Inquiry. Instead she walked down the corridor containing the short row
of vice presidential offices. As she walked, she thought of
John Thatcher's raised finger, she thought of the electric
chair, she thought of many past kindnesses and four years
of comradeship.

She knocked politely on the door.

"Come in," called the low, easy voice of Jay Rutledge.

Without faltering, Mary Sullivan went in.

# 20

# *Exeunt Omnes*

John Thatcher did not see any of the people from National Calculating until four days after Jay Rutledge's spectacular suicide from the sixteenth floor of the Southern Bourbon Building had halted traffic on Madison Avenue and sent five passersby scurrying to the phone, fearing that the bottom had dropped out of the market, and the dark days of 1929 had returned. He had, however, followed events in the press.

*The New York Times* was having a field day. Always eager to instruct its readers, that worthy journal had abandoned both its aversion to crime and its spirited attempt to instill the rudiments of Laotian geography into one million New Yorkers in favor of the intricacies of cost accounting and government procurement practices. Scarcely a day passed without a painstaking definition of "break-even" costs making the front page. Detailed analyses of Rutledge's accounts, elaborate maps of his double warehouse system in New Jersey, and a biography of the president of the American Society of Certified Public Accountants absorbed substantial portions of the first section.

The *Wall Street Journal* renounced the pleasures of technical detail, and devoted itself to weighty speculations concerning the future of the TCR, the survival of National Calculating, and the career of General Cartwright. "With the high rate of fall-out in the computer industry, more than one competitor of National Calculating is considering the possibility of offering bids to the U.S. Army for the TCR contract. This contract, at a properly negotiated price, could mean the difference between life and death for many new entrants in the field, bedeviled by rising labor costs and substantial research and development expenditures." The *Journal* went on to reassure its subscribers as to the future of conventional armament. "No doubt about it, feeling on Capitol Hill is running in favor of continuance of the heavy artillery support program in spite of the National Calculating scandal. 'It still hasn't cost as much as the development of The Boomerang,' one Congressman is reported as saying. The Boomerang is the missile that broke loose from its radar control over Florida last year, attacking and destroying a heavy bomber carrying seven men." But the *Journal* did fear that the fraud would be seized on by left-wing sympathizers to undermine the public's faith in the probity of American business. "It is unfortunate," they concluded, "that by his actions, a man like Jay Rutledge can subject thousands of upright and honest executives to renewed attacks by labor leaders and publicity-conscious Democratic jobholders. We are confident, however, that public opinion will rally behind the chief victims of this fraud—the management of National Calculating."

Curiously enough, public opinion was providing some support for the beleaguered forces at National. The elaborate concealment of his fraud by Jay Rutledge coupled with the prompt resignation of Charles Mason had scotched suggestions of collusion by the front office. But while gratifying, this public sentiment did not relieve the company of its obligations to the government. Successive invasions had swept through National Calculating. First the police, then the FBI, and finally the examiners from the Government Accounting Office. The latest estimate established the corporation's liability at approximately one hundred million dollars. The Sloan Guaranty Trust, together with Robichaux and Devane, had issued bracing statements of confidence—and then retired to write off their respective investments. All this was enough to depress the most robust management group in the world. It was with some surprise, therefore, that Thatcher found himself on the following Friday evening at a party in Morris Richter's apartment which, while certainly subdued, was not radiating that sense of impending doom he had come to associate with the senior echelons of National Calculating.

"Well, I still don't understand what happened," complained Tom Robichaux, holding out his glass absently for Morris Richter to refill. "And furthermore," he continued, mildly indignant, "it doesn't seem fair that I should miss the grand finale when you consider all that I put up with before."

A good many of those present agreed with him. The swift and unexpected conclusion of their mystery, and the subsequent mobilization of all forces to salvage whatever possible from the debacle had prevented almost everyone at National Calculating from finding out what really happened. They simply knew that Jay Rutledge had been cooking his books until Clarence Fortinbras caught him at it.

"It's not surprising that we were all fooled," mused Thatcher, who looked wildly improbable sitting in a chair made of rope and canvas which was unexpectedly comfortable. "We were all looking for the wrong thing. We expected to find someone who was lining his own pockets. Nobody was. Instead, Rutledge was robbing the Army and putting the money into the company's till."

Harry Blaney, who had been invited to the gathering for old times' sake, nodded his satisfaction. "I never could see how he was making a profit. It didn't seem possible."

"It isn't," agreed Thatcher. "But he knew nothing you said would be taken very seriously. Everybody expects an unsuccessful division manager to make excuses. That was the real strength of his position. Nobody examines the successful part of a business to find out what's wrong. You look to the unsuccessful parts. The only thing he had to fear was Blaney's insistence on a division comparison to improve his own performance, and Rutledge got out of that by wrapping himself in a cloak of government security and refusing flatly to divulge his division statistics."

"Why?"

Everybody turned to look. Josie Richter, their hostess, was sitting cross-legged on the floor atop a large purple cushion, and up to now had been a silent spectator. She repeated her question.

"Why did he bother? What good did it do him to rob the Army?"

"It did him a great deal of good," said Blaney kindly. "It got him a salary of forty thousand dollars a year, a healthy bunch of stock options, and a pension of twenty thousand a year socked away for the future. Rutledge would have been nothing if it hadn't been for that contract."

"Poor Jay," said Margaret Cobb to the group at large. She smiled at their surprise. "He was always afraid of being just nothing. You know, we came to National together. The TCR was developed when we were both still in the research laboratories. Then the Korean War came, and he got a chance to go into the production end as assistant division manager in charge of TCR production. He grabbed it. And, of course, he did so well he just took over the division. All along he was determined not to end up as a permanent assistant in Research and Development." There was no sting in her words. Everybody knew that Margaret Cobb had accepted the job of division manager for R&D which a harassed Board of Directors had been only too happy to offer her.

"He must have started his swindle way back then. After all, he was the one who worked out the original specifications," reflected Morris Richter thoughtfully. He was standing by the fireplace, leaning against the mantel. "It wouldn't be hard. In fact, it's what I said all along. Either Harry was paying too much on costs or Jay was paying too little. But I was too blind to see which was happening. That Jay was really selling second-hand goods at first-hand prices."

Blaney smiled broad-mindedly. He was very pleased with himself for having left National Calculating before the sentimental claims of crisis could impede his departure. "Everybody was blind," he said good-humoredly. "That is, everybody except Fortinbras maybe." He looked a question at Margaret Cobb.

"Yes, Clarence was finding out—piecing things together bit by bit. There's no doubt about it," she agreed. "I had a long talk with Emily yesterday. She says that he was very enthusiastic toward the end. He kept telling her that, if the books at Commercial Sales were all right, then that left only one possibility. It didn't mean anything to her, of course. But he must have stated the same two possibilities that Morris has. Clarence, you see, really would have been enthusiastic if he had come across a fraud like this. He would have been delighted to realize that everybody else had been misled by the success of Jay's division. Clarence was one of those rare men who bring to their profession all the zeal the rest of us keep for private pleasures. He was a *passionate* accountant—that's really the only word for it." She paused reminiscently for a moment. "I began to see a faint glimmer on that last day, when Jay quarreled with me about talking to General Cartwright. For the first time I remembered Clarence had really finished with Harry's books when he began to talk about fraud and a physical inventory in New Jersey. But I didn't understand what it all meant. You did," she concluded, looking at Thatcher with approval.

"There's no doubt that what Fortinbras meant to do was to go over to the plant and check the inventory of parts for the TCR's" said Thatcher. "And Rutledge was quite right in his assessment of the situation. Once Fortinbras had gotten that far, nothing but his death could keep Rutledge out of jail."

"Then why all that business of stealing some of the records from Fortinbras's office?" asked Richter.

"That was before Fortinbras announced his plans for physical inventory," replied Thatcher, shifting cautiously in his chair. It held. "Some of his current division records on purchases had been sent to Fortinbras before he had a chance to make them coincide with his requirements. Normally, of course, he fudged his records long before any auditor got to see them. While he was in Fortinbras's office, taking what he wanted, he took a lot of other material at random so as to confuse the issue. Incidentally we had a clue a long time ago that we never understood. Unfortunately, I think that Stanley Draper did understand it."

"Thank God they have pulled him through," Mrs. Cobb said fervently while Morris Richter circulated among his guests with refills and canapés. Richter had been unusually thoughtful ever since the Chairman of the Board had called to offer him Rutledge's job. He had asked for a day to think it over, and eventually his acceptance had been relayed to the board. He was now trying to adjust to the position of heading a division which had just defrauded its only customer to the tune of a hundred million dollars. "Look at it as a challenge, my boy!" urged the Chairman who was desperate for someone to fill the job. Richter had looked, and was therefore suffering a certain dejection of spirit.

Under cover of the general stir, Robichaux leaned forward to tap Josie Richter urgently on the shoulder.

"You said that Katrina would be here," he said reproachfully.

Josie smiled knowingly. "She's coming," she whispered at him, "but she said she had to stop for something."

Thatcher had nodded at Mrs. Cobb's comment. "I don't suppose that it can ever be definitely proved that Rutledge pushed young Draper in front of that car," he said.

"But what does Draper know that made him so dangerous?"

"Yes," said Allen Hammond. "And what is this clue that we didn't understand?"

Hammond had arrived earlier with a subdued Mary Sullivan. This was her first public appearance since she had precipitated Jay Rutledge's final desperate act. Her activity had been rewarded with a decisive martial rebuke from General Cartwright which she had borne with great composure, offering no excuse other than her friendship with the dead man. But after being taken home by Allen Hammond, she had remained in seclusion until this evening, turning a deaf ear to Mason's pleas for assistance in winding up his affairs. It was generally accepted that Hammond had been her constant companion during this period, and their appearance together had caused no comment other than Josie Richter's muttered aside to her husband about a certain chafing dish. The Richters had suffered from a surfeit of chafing dishes ever since their own marriage eight years earlier.

"You have to go back to the day the papers were stolen," said Thatcher in reply to Hammond's question. "Rutledge at that time still had no thought of murder. After all, he had survived a number of audits since he started his fraud. His paper record was as perfect as a paper record can be. Most accountants don't undertake an audit in the spirit of a crusade. Their job is to make sure that the financial statements adequately reflect the condition of the company . . . that's all." Thatcher frowned as he remembered his long talk the previous day with Addison, the bank's accountant, who had assured him that the fraud would never have been caught by an ordinary audit. "If the company is doing badly, then the statements have to show the company is doing badly. But they're not responsible for finding out why. For instance, if Mr. Blaney had been paying too much for his supplies, their only concern would be that the high price of his supplies be stated for everyone to see. So Rutledge was not too concerned. But he had heard enough about Fortinbras's peculiar talents to be mildly apprehensive and to resist giving him access to the books. Then Fortinbras, instead of sitting quietly back and letting the divisions send him their books, started sending out messengers and raiding the files. That way he obtained records Rutledge had not yet fixed. So Rutledge simply stole them. By the time he was called on to produce duplicates, he would have conformed them to his requirements. But he was nervous enough about the theft to make his first mistake."

Thatcher looked around at his audience which was now silently attentive. Everybody was very tired. The last few days had involved a major reorganization at National Calculating which had been touched off by Chip Mason's resignation and, ramifying downwards, had altered the status of practically every employee. Allen Hammond's last-minute bid for the presidency had failed. He had had to be content with elevation to Blaney's job as manager of Commercial

Sales. The Board of Directors, after an uninterrupted session of eight hours, had offered the chief executive position to the Controller, who had ridden out the entire storm in Elkhart, Indiana—apparently on the theory that only physical isolation provided any guarantee against contamination from the irregularities manifest in National's front office. It would be days before the Controller had his team ready to swing into action and start a salvage operation.

"Rutledge knew that there would be some sort of scene when Fortinbras returned to the office and discovered the missing papers," continued Thatcher. "And he didn't want to be there. So he simply went out and stayed out for several hours. When he returned, the scene was over, and he could pretend ignorance of the whole situation."

"I remember that," remarked Blaney. "He skipped out for lunch with Cartwright and by the middle of the next week he still hadn't heard that Fortinbras accused me of stealing the papers."

"But that's the whole point." Thatcher raised an admonitory finger. "He didn't have lunch with Cartwright. You were all so used to having him disappear for hours in order to shepherd the General around that none of you questioned it. But two things came out of that little episode. First of all, Fortinbras was stung into sufficient anger that he went over the history and records of Blaney's division with such vituperative care that he succeeded in convincing himself that there was nothing wrong at all with Commercial Sales. Which made him very deeply suspicious of Government Contracts doing the same work at a much greater profit. And second, Rutledge—who really was mad on the subject of having a perfect paper record—tried to buttress his alibi of lunching with Cartwright by turning in an expense chit for the meal. And now we come to Stanley Draper. Because, of course, that expense chit was eventually reviewed by Draper in closing out his accounts."

"Well, what difference did that make?" asked Robichaux testily. He was getting very bored with the whole thing. He had come only because Josie Richter had assured him of Katrina's presence. Instead he was hearing a long lecture on a company he intended to expunge from his memory as rapidly as possible. Devane had been markedly unsympathetic about the whole affair.

"Now, Tom. You remember Hammond told us that Fortinbras's explosion over the robbery of his office was interrupted by Barney Young's appearing with cigars to celebrate the birth of his son that morning. Well, the night I met Rutledge and Cartwright at the Biltmore, Cartwright told me about having lunch with Young the day his son was born. He even helped him buy the cigars. You can see what happened. Young, of course, also put in a chit for that lunch. By the time Stanley Draper reviewed the expense accounts, Fortinbras was dead. But he had inspired the boy with his own enthusiasm for tracking down discrepancies. Draper contacted Rutledge to straighten out the confusion over that lunch. We know that from Rutledge's secretary. Draper left a message with her that he wanted to see Rutledge about his expense accounts. And Rutledge made an appointment with him. I gather that young Draper is still confused about things, but he remembers all of that very clearly."

"But that can't be all," protested Morris Richter. "It's such a little thing. Nobody would commit murder for that."

"No, it isn't such a little thing. Remember, Draper was in the office next to Fortinbras's during two critical periods, the murder and the robbery. Rutledge was probably very sensitive about that. He might have been afraid that Draper had seen him. Then, Draper tackled him about the luncheon alibi. From what you yourself said, Richter, Stanley wasn't easy to intimidate in his own field. He probably told Rutledge that some sort of adjustment would have to be made in the expense accounts. Rutledge, of course, must have assumed that the significance of the date would dawn on Draper any moment. The boy had been present during Fortinbras's tantrum, it had been a dramatic episode; and to Young, of course, it was a red-letter day, incapable of being confused with any other day. And finally, I'm afraid that we inadvertently nearly sent young Draper to his death. The day after we had spoken to you," and Thatcher waved a hand toward the kitchen, "we showed up at National Calculating while Regina Plout was there. In front of Rutledge, we announced that we wanted to talk to Stanley Draper. For all he knew, Draper might have asked to see us. Rutledge had already committed a major fraud and one murder to stay out of jail. He simply wasn't taking any chances. I don't think there's any doubt that he followed Stanley Draper from the office that evening and pushed him under the first available car."

"But he's going to be all right?" Josie Richter asked.

"He's even cheerful," her husband said absently. "He's getting promoted."

Margaret Cobb looked at them. "And Emily is going to give him Clarence's library," she said. "Stanley told her it was worth being pushed under a car for."

The smiles greeting this news faded into a sober silence. Jay Rutledge had chosen murder and suicide in preference to exposure. It is not pleasant to think that a man you have worked with and known as an ordinary, kindly human being has been hiding a near-mad desperation. A ghost seemed to walk the room.

Allen Hammond was determined to give the conversation a cheerier turn. "By the way, whatever happened to Regina Plout?"

"Didn't you hear?" Morris Richter welcomed the change of subject. "She's written to Chip. Apologized and said she realizes he was taken in by that man with the shifty eyes."

"What's old Chip up to these days?" inquired Blaney lazily, stretching himself on the sofa.

Hammond grinned. "Uncle Chas has retired from business. He's heading up the drive for the Harvard Athletic Fund. They want to build a new stadium."

"What's wrong with the one they've got?" asked Richter innocently.

"It only holds thirty-eight thousand people," replied Hammond gravely.

"Oh."

Amidst the respectful silence that ensued, the peal of the bell was clearly heard. Josie Richter, with a knowing smile at Robichaux, went to answer the door. Thatcher, from sheer force of habit, directed a censorious frown toward his volatile comrade.

"No, no!" protested Robichaux in a sibilant whisper. "You've got it all wrong, John."

"Have I?" Thatcher was ironical.

"Dammit, my intentions are honorable!"

Thatcher sighed. That was the trouble with Tom's intentions. They always were.

"Old Barnwell wouldn't like this at all," he said heavily.

"Oh, that's all right." Tom reassured him. "The divorce has been finalized. Not a bad woman, Dorothy—in her own way, that is," he added tolerantly.

Both men rose to their feet to greet the newcomer. But she was not alone. Towering over his escort, who shepherded him into the room like an intelligent sheepdog, Georgi Borof acknowledged Thatcher's presence with huge delight.

"This is a celebration, everybody," announced Katrina Tametz, attaching herself firmly to Robichaux, "and we've brought champagne. Georgi is going on television!"

The gathering responded dutifully. They crowded around the enormous Albanian, patting him on the shoulder, making proper inquiries, shouting congratulations. Champagne corks popped; glasses were produced; toasts were proposed.

People eddied about, resettling themselves into new groups. Robichaux led Katrina to a couch where she sat down beside him, looking up with great soulful dark eyes. "How sad that now you should be all alone in the world," she murmured.

Allen Hammond moved over to the arm of Mary Sullivan's chair. "See," he said. "It wasn't so bad, was it? You can't go on staying locked up at home." She smiled up at him. He covered her hand with his. "Not that there isn't a lot to be said for your staying at home. But in a different way entirely." Their two heads moved close together as their voices dropped to a whisper.

Morris and Josie Richter retreated to a window alcove for a *sotto voce* conversation concerning the liquor supply, and whether or not scrambled eggs would be required. "We have only a dozen," Josie hissed. "You'll have to get some more when you go out for Scotch."

Margaret Cobb took a second glass of champagne and recklessly confided to Blaney her long-cherished plans for the future of Research and Development. But Blaney wanted to tell her about Southern Midwest Electric. "Utilities are booming in the central states, Margaret. Why, the population increase around Chicago alone—"

Georgi Borof settled himself on the floor by Thatcher's chair, with a bottle of champagne within comfortable reach.

"And now, Mr. Thatcher," he said silkily, "now, I sing for you."

Thatcher closed his eyes as the opening chords of the balalaika were wafted across the room.